Speaking of Murder

A Melodrama in Three Acts

Audrey and William Roos

A SAMUEL FRENCH ACTING EDITION

SAMUEL FRENCH
FOUNDED 1830

SAMUELFRENCH.COM
SAMUELFRENCH-LONDON.CO.UK

FOR PRODUCTION ENQUIRIES

UNITED STATES AND CANADA

Info@SamuelFrench.com

1-866-598-8449

UNITED KINGDOM AND EUROPE

Plays@SamuelFrench-London.co.uk

020-7255-4302

Each title is subject to availability from Samuel French, depending upon
country of performance. Please be aware that *SPEAKING OF MURDER*
may not be licensed by Samuel French in your territory. Professional
and amateur producers should contact the nearest Samuel French
office or licensing partner to verify availability.

Please refer to page 92 for further copyright information.

SPEAKING OF MURDER was first presented by Courtney Burr and Burgess Meredith at the Royale Theatre, New York City, on December 19, 1956, with the following cast:

(IN ORDER OF APPEARANCE)

RICKY ASHTON	*Billy Quinn*
CONNIE BARNES ASHTON	*Neva Patterson*
JANIE ASHTON	*Virginia Gerry*
CHARLES ASHTON	*Lorne Greene*
ANNABELLE LOGAN	*Brenda de Banzie*
MRS. WALWORTH	*Estelle Winwood*
MILDRED	*Brook Byron*
MITCHELL	*Robert Mandan*

Directed by Delbert Mann

Setting and Lighting by Frederick Fox

Costumes by Alice Gibson

TIME: The Present.

PLACE: The entire action of the play takes place in the library of the Ashton home, forty miles north of New York City.

SCENES

ACT ONE

SCENE I: *Late afternoon, early July.*

SCENE II: *Half an hour later.*

ACT TWO

SCENE I: *The following Friday, shortly before noon.*

SCENE II: *Later that afternoon.*

ACT THREE

The same afternoon, five o'clock.

3

Speaking of Murder

ACT ONE

SCENE I

The Ashton library is a large, high-ceilinged room in a rock castle of a house on the east bank of the Hudson River, north of Tarrytown. It is indeed a library. The walls are lined with book-filled shelves from floor to ceiling. There is a tall library ladder. There is a door in the Right wall, leading to the children's wing. In the Center of the rear wall there are narrow louvered double doors, apparently a closet. To the Left of it is the door to the hall. The Left side wall of the room is almost completely taken up by French doors, opening on a terrace. There is a desk with a chair before it and behind it just inside the terrace doors. Behind the desk in the rear wall there is a small cupboard built into the shelves. In the Center of the room there is a long sofa, a coffee table before it, other chairs flanking the table. There is a huge antique grandfather's clock. A very feminine effort has been made to "cozy up" the old-fashioned austerity of the room with chintzes and other gay fabrics.

As the Curtain rises a small dog is resting comfortably on the sofa. RICKY ASHTON, a boy of nine, is sitting in a wing-back chair, reading a book. After a moment RICKY suddenly closes the book, rises. He goes to the sofa, sits beside the dog, rubs its ears.

RICKY. Hello, Joe, what do you know?

(RICKY *rises, wanders to desk. Bored, he idly dials phone without lifting receiver. The clock strikes four. The phone dial gives* RICKY *an idea. He makes sure that no one is coming, then runs to the louvered doors. He opens the doors disclosing the steel door of a walk-in vault. He dials the cobination, swings open the heavy door—then hears someone in the hall. In his haste to get away he doesn't get the vault door or the louvered doors completely closed. He runs out to the terrace, disappears.* CONNIE BARNES, *a strikingly beautiful, dark-haired young woman in her early thirties, enters from the hall. She puts her purse and gloves on the coffee table, sits on sofa. wearily.*)

CONNIE. *(Petting the dog)* Hello, Joe, what do you know?

(JANIE ASHTON, *a robust little girl of seven, enters Right. She wears shorts and a T-shirt.*)

JANIE. Hi, Connie!
CONNIE. Hiya, Janie. Where are you going in such a rush?
JANIE. I'm going to help Ricky paint his boat. Miss Annabelle said I could. *(She heads for the terrace, then turns back)* Connie, Beverly Hills has been calling you all afternoon.
CONNIE. *(Sighs)* Thanks, Janie. Is your father in the studio?
JANIE. I think so.
CONNIE. Will you tell him I'm home?
JANIE. Okay! *(She exits.)*

(CONNIE *pats dog for a moment, then the PHONE rings. It rings again before she answers it.*)

CONNIE. *(Into phone)* Hello— Mrs. Ashton? *(She sees* CHARLES ASHTON *coming across the terrace)* Just a moment, I'll see—

(Charles enters. He is an attractive man, about forty.)

Charles. Connie! How did you get home?

Connie. I got a lift. Darling, it's California again—tell them I'm not here—anything— *(She hands the phone to him.)*

Charles. *(Into phone, enjoying the situation)* Hello, this is Mr. Ashton. Yes, Operator— I know you do, but she's not here. She's gone on a trip somewhere. Hudson Bay, I think—won't be back for months. Sorry— Goodbye. *(He hangs up, laughs)* California may never call again.

Connie. Darling, I've made that picture eighteen times. There's always this girl singer—or dancer—or skater or swimmer—who comes to New York—and I'm always her roommate! Charles, I want to be your roommate!

Charles. *(Taking her in his arms)* Glad to have you, stick around, make yourself comfortable—

(They kiss, then break apart as Annabelle Logan enters from hall. She is a pretty blonde, nearly forty. She is English. She carries a handful of mail.)

Annabelle. Connie, why on earth did you walk home? I saw you from my window—

Charles. You walked home? You said you got a ride.

Connie. *(A little laugh)* That wasn't quite accurate— I did walk.

Annabelle. Three miles! In those heels!

Charles. Why the hell didn't you call me?

Annabelle. Yes! You were to call Charles when you finished at the hairdressers.

Connie. *(Reluctantly)* I did. I talked to Ricky. *(To Charles)* He said he'd tell you I was ready to come home and I started walking to meet you. Apparently Ricky forgot to tell you.

Charles. He forgot to tell me?

Connie. I'm sure that's all it was!

Annabelle. Of course it is! The child's so excited about his boat he can't think of anything else. Connie, the photographer's going to be here at five sharp. That should give you and Charles plenty of time to get to your cocktail party.

CONNIE. *(Sits on sofa)* Don't worry about that.

ANNABELLE. The ladies are thrilled that you're going to pose with them! With you in the picture we'll make the front page. Charles, it was so very clever of you to marry a movie star.

CHARLES. I'd do anything for the Visiting Nurses.

ANNABELLE. Connie, I want you to know how grateful—

CONNIE. I'm not doing anything—but, you, you've been knocking yourself out for this auction.

(CHARLES *notices that the louvered doors are ajar; he goes to them.)*

ANNABELLE. I can't bear the thought of the Visiting Nurses being without funds. They do such good work.

CHARLES. The vault's open! My God! Who did that?

ANNABELLE. *(Quickly)* I'm afraid I did—

CHARLES. *(He closes steel door)* Leaving this thing open is like leaving a loaded gun around.

ANNABELLE. I know and I'm sorry. I only meant to leave the room for a second. I'm sorry, Charles.

CONNIE. *(Rises)* What's all the fuss about?

CHARLES. *(Closing louvered doors)* I got caught in there once when I was a kid. It scared hell out of me. That damn vault is sound-proof, fire-proof, dust-proof, air-proof—

ANNABELLE. And moth-proof. Connie, I thought you might store your furs there.

CHARLES. Where did you find the combination? I haven't see it for years.

ANNABELLE. In the desk. It's always been there. I was just checking to see if the vault needed cleaning.

CONNIE. It was built for furs? What's it doing here in the library?

CHARLES. It wasn't built for furs. My father built it for

his rare book collection. *(Moves to desk)* The vault cost so much to build he never could afford any rare books.

ANNABELLE. Connie, I don't mean to rush, but it's time you were changing.

CONNIE. You're right, I'd better start dressing.

ANNABELLE. Oh, Connie, there's some mail for you—and for you, Charles.

CONNIE. *(Picks up dog, purse and gloves)* Thanks, I'll see it later. I've got to feed my starving hound before I dress. *(Exits to hall.)*

CHARLES. *(Starting after her)* I'll feed your starving hound.

ANNABELLE. *(Halting CHARLES by holding out mail for him)* Oh, Charles?

CHARLES. Yes? *(Takes mail, moves back to desk.)*

ANNABELLE. About Ricky and the phone call—you don't really think it was intentional? That he deliberately didn't give you Connie's message?

CHARLES. Three weeks ago I couldn't imagine Ricky doing that to anyone. Now—I don't know.

ANNABELLE. I'm certain it was accidental. Oh, there's no denying that he hasn't been very friendly to Connie, but—

CHARLES. Friendly! He's been sniping at her ever since she got here! He's made her life miserable.

ANNABELLE. Oh, Charles, Connie understands—

CHARLES. How can she? I don't! When the kids were out on the coast they fell in love with her.

ANNABELLE. Of course they did!

CHARLES. Then what's happened?

ANNABELLE. Children resent change, it frightens them. And you know how secure they've been. We've never had any problems. They were completely happy here with us—weren't they, Charles?

CHARLES. I've really handed Connie a job. *(Sits.)*

ANNABELLE. It's going to be all right. *(Going to desk, gets letter)* I'm sure of it—so sure that I've made my reservations! The *Queen Mary*, a week from Friday. Imagine, after all these years, I'm going to London once again!

CHARLES. A week from Friday—well, Annabelle—

ANNABLELE. No, don't make me a farewell speech! Not yet—there's plenty of time for that!

CHARLES. I'm not going to—but you know how grateful I am. We couldn't ahve done without you these last three years. Since Elizabeth died—

ANNABELLE. Elizabeth was my friend. To look after her children, your children, I wanted to do that. It's been the most exciting experience of my life. I only wish I could have done a better job preparing them for Connie.

CHARLES. I didn't give you very much time for that.

ANNABELLE. Yes, you did yet married rather suddenly, didn't you? Still— I might have done more.

CHARLES. Annabelle. *(He rises)* This is our problem now— *(Steps to* ANNABELLE*)* Connie's and mine. We shouldn't depend on you any longer.

ANNABELLE. I suppose not. You know it hasn't been easy for me to stay on here. But I simply had to, even though I knew my presence here must be an embarrassment to you.

CHARLES. Annabelle—

ANNABELLE. No, Charles, it's all right. We're not going into all that again. But I do wish you would realize that our little interlude—was no more than that. It meant no more to me than it did to you. You were lonely —and I was so available.

CHARLES. *(Taking her hand)* Annabelle—

ANNABELLE. Charles, forgive me. *(She puts her other hand on his)* But I do want you to know that I think Connie is perfect for you, and you know I wish you both the best of everything—

(CHARLES *kisses her on cheek.*)

JANIE. *(Off Left)* He's in here, Ricky! *(She runs on through the terrace doors.)*

(CHARLES *steps back as she comes to them.*)

Hey, Daddy! (JANIE *has paint on her face, hands and jersey. She is rubbing at paint with a rag.*)

CHARLES. Oh, no!

ANNABELLE. Janie, what on earth!

JANIE. Ricky doesn't have any turpentine. He said Daddy might.

CHARLES. Daddy better have some— (*He takes* JANIE *gingerly by the corner of her jersey*) Or we'll just have to throw Janie away.

(*They start for terrace.*)

Come on, baby. I'll take care of you.

(*They exit.*)

How did such a little girl get so much paint all over her.

ANNABELLE. (*Watches them go, puts letter on desk, then turns and starts for hall. She stops, noticing vault. She opens steel door. She goes to terrace doors and steps out*) Ricky! Oh, Ricky, come here a moment, will you? (*She comes back into room to wait for* RICKY)

(*He enters.*)

Ricky!

RICKY. Yes, Miss Annabelle?

ANNABELLE. (*Indicating the open vault*) Ricky—

RICKY. Oh—

ANNABELLE. Yes, dear, Oh. (*Sits in chair below desk*)

(*He faces her.*)

The reason I never told your father you knew the combination was because you promised me you'd never play with the vault unless I was here in the room with you.

RICKY. I know that—

ANNABELLE. But you have been playing with it—not just today, either. Often, haven't you?

RICKY. Yes, Miss Annabelle.

ANNABELLE. I understand the fascination it has for you. It is fun, working the combination, isn't it?

RICKY. Yes, Miss Annabelle.

ANNABELLE. Well, close the door now, Ricky, and then you and I will make an agreement.

(RICKY *runs to vault, closes the steel door and spins*

the dial.)
Close it up tightly.
(RICKY *closes the louvered doors.)*
That's a good boy.
(He comes down to her.)
Ricky dear, I won't be here to take care of you much longer.

RICKY. Yes, you will! You're not going.

ANNABELLE. A week from Friday—

RICKY. No!

ANNABELLE. I must, and I want you to make me a brand new promise, and this time keep it. So Miss Annabelle doesn't worry about you when she's far away in London. Promise me you will never open that vault without permission.

RICKY. Okay.

ANNABELLE. I promise, Miss Annabelle.

RICKY. I promise, Miss Annabelle.

ANNABELLE. All right, you may run along now.

RICKY. Thank you, Miss Annabelle. *(He exits, running, through terrace doors.)*

ANNABELLE. *(Waits a moment, then goes to vault, checks that no one is watching, and opens louvered doors. She expertly dials the combination and swings open the steel door. She glances around the room for a moment, then she exits out through the hall doors and off Left. Off-stage)* Joe— Here Joe. C'mon Joe. *(She re-enters through hall doors with* CONNIE'S *dog in her arms, patting it and talking to it. She goes to vault)* Nice Joe. Nice little doggie. Nice boy. *(With a final pat she puts the dog in the vault, shuts the door, spins the dial and closes the louvered doors. She then starts for door Right.)*

JANIE. *(On terrace)* Miss Annabelle, look! Mrs. Walworth is here!

(JANIE *leads* MRS. WALWORTH *in.* ETHEL WALWORTH *is over fifty, but fighting not to look forty. It is a losing battle; her appearance is rather odd—so is her manner. She has a shabby elegance about her that is almost comic. She is English. She wears a huge sum-mer hat and carries a gaudy, old-fashioned parasol. JANIE is fascinated by her; she keeps inspecting her.)*

MRS. WALWORTH. Annabelle, my dear!

ANNABELLE. *(Surprised, and definitely not pleased)* Mrs. Walworth—well!

MRS. WALWORTH. Yes! Such a day! Lovely! The path through the woods, you know *(She looks at* JANIE) The image of her mother when Elizabeth was her age. God bless you, my dear.

JANIE. Thank you! God bless you, too.

MRS. WALWORTH. Now, now, children should be seen and not heard. I so enjoyed taking care of your mother when she was little. In London, that was. Do you know where London is?

*(*JANIE *nods.)*

And often I took care of your Miss Annabelle when she came to play with your mummy. Did you know that?

*(*JANIE *nods.)*

Cat got your tongue? *(She seats herself comfortably, turns to* ANNABELLE) Well—just a bit of sherry, perhaps. Or if that's too much trouble, a gin and tonic. *(To* JANIE) Run, my dear, ask Mildred to bring me a gin and tonic, light on the tonic. Run, child!

*(*JANIE *exits to hall.)*

*(*MRS. WALWORTH *turns, watches* JANIE *leave, then turns back to* ANNABELLE) Well, I must say, Annabelle, you've brought her up properly. Where's the new mother?

ANNABELLE. *(Coldly)* Oh, so you want to see our movie star! That's what brought you here.

MRS. WALWORTH. Not entirely. Though I do admire her, if you like that type. Been married before, didn't you say, off and on?

ANNABELLE. Just once. When she was much too young. There was a divorce.

MRS. WALWORTH. And perhaps there'll be another. Don't despair, he may just tire of her and you'll be a

Queen-Bee here once again. When do they start to build the new house?

ANNABELLE. Soon, quite soon. *(Sits on sofa.)*

MRS. WALWORTH. Does she insist? No, she wouldn't have to, if I know Mr. Ashton. Even though it's been in his family—for how many generations—he wouldn't want her living here—in the shadow of Elizabeth's tragedy. How much better they should start fresh in a nice fresh house all their own.

ANNABELLE. Charles has always meant to build. This old monstrosity of a place is hardly an advertisement for a modern architect.

MRS. WALWORTH. *(Grinning)* You prefer to think that's it. So galling for you—that it isn't to be your new house, yours and his.

ANNABELLE. *(Evenly)* Just what brought you here today?

MRS. WALWORTH. I thought I'd save you a trip this week, my dear. It must be so very tiresome for you— trudging over to my dull little cottage week after week.

ANNABELLE. It's a charming cottage.

MRS. WALWORTH. But so expensive. I don't know, I'm not extravagant, but I don't seem able to manage.

ANNABELLE. You're extravagant, my dear.

MRS. WALWORTH. Am I, really? Well, if I am, we just must face up to it. But at the moment—a small advance would be so appreciated.

ANNABELLE. I'll bring you your forty dollars on Friday. As usual.

MRS. WALWORTH. You are uncooperative.

ANNABELLE. We have an agreement—and you must learn to manage.

MRS. WALWORTH. You've no idea how much lonelier one is when one has no money to speak of—

MILDRED. *(A maid in her twenties, enters from hall with a gin and tonic on a tray)* Here you are, Mrs. Walworth.

MRS. WALWORTH. *(Taking the glass)* Thank you, my dear.

MILDRED. Would you like a cup of tea, Miss Annabelle?

ANNABELLE. Not at the moment, thank you, Mildred. But you might put the kettle on.

MILDRED. *(Going)* Yes, Miss Annabelle.

MRS. WALWORTH. *(To* MILDRED*)* Yes, do put the kettle on, but don't put the gin away!

ANNABELLE. And close the door, please, Mildred.

(MILDRED *closes hall door after her.*)

MRS. WALWORTH. A pretty girl, Mildred, in a dull sort of way. Has she many boys?

ANNABELLE. A few, I think.

MRS. WALWORTH. How far does she let them go?

ANNABELLE. Mrs. Walworth, did you ever have any taste at all? I don't remember.

MRS. WALWORTH. I don't recall, either. But I'm afraid not. It comes from being around children so much. That's one thing I like about the little ones—their vulgarity. *(She notices cigarette case on coffee-table. Puts drink down and picks up the case)* What a handsome case. "C.B." Connie Barnes. My, my, Cartier's. Mr. Ashton give it to her?

ANNABELLE. No, she's had it before that.

MRS. WALWORTH. Must be worth a pretty penny. Three hundred dollars? Even more? Four hundred. Five?

ANNABELLE. I've no idea. Put it down, my dear.

MRS. WALWORTH. Such a handsome thing. Makes one wish one smoked. I suppose one could learn. *(She opens purse, drops the cigarette case inside.)*

ANNABELLE. *(Quietly)* Put it back where you found it, dear.

MRS. WALWORTH. *(Significantly)* I had another letter from Lucinda Marsh—you remember litle Lucinda—

ANNABELLE. Don't bother going through that again. Really, you can be so very tiresome.

MRS. WALWORTH. I'm just as bored with it as you are, my dear. But unfortunately, it does seem necessary every so often to refresh your memory about Lucinda and her letters.

ANNABELLE. But I can't let you have your way this time. How shall I explain it?

MRS. WALWORTH. Easily, my dear. You're so clever. You were always the clever one. Elizabeth the pretty one, who got all the boys. And Lucinda was the thoughtful one. I only took care of her a year or so after I left Elizabeth. But she still writes to me! After all these years! How very thoughtful. *(She takes blue air mail letter from purse as* ANNABELLE *rises)* Her writing hasn't improved since she was nine— *(She reads)* "—and give all my love to little Beebee.
It must be such a comfort to Mr. Ashton that Beebee is still there. I can imagine how wonderful she is with the children. I should like a snapshot of little Ricky and Jane. Do they resemble their mother? Elizabeth was the prettiest girl—"

ANNABELLE. *(Turning to her)* Must you? I was never a great admirer of Lucinda's letters! *(She moves to desk, picks up letter opener.)*

MRS. WALWORTH. You're right it is a dull letter, very dull. Except that some people think Beebee was Elizabeth's nickname. That isn't dull. Is it, Beebee?

ANNABELLE. *(Slams down letter opener and goes quickly to* MRS. WALWORTH*)* Don't! Don't call me that!

MRS. WALWORTH. *(Quickly moving letter away from* ANNABELLE*)* Oh, no, my dear, it wouldn't do you any good to take this letter from me. You know that. I have dozens of them and God willing I shall get dozens more. Sit down, Annabelle, and don't make it necessary for me to call you Beebee.

> (ANNABELLE *hesitates, then slowly sits in wing-chair.)*

How will you explain it? I'm curious. About the cigarette case, I mean. Please don't blame it on the servants. Someone was telling me only recently that in Charles' father's day there were fifteen here in help—

ANNABELLE. *(Turning to her quietly)* I'm not at all sure I'm going to let you take that case.

MRS. WALWORTH. Really, my dear, can't we consider that settled?

ANNABELLE. I'm not at all sure. *(She rises, extends hand to* MRS. WALWORTH*)* Give it to me, or I shall call Connie down.

MRS. WALWORTH. How tiresome you can be, Annabelle. You were as a child too—so persistent— Persistence isn't charming you know.

ANNABELLE. *(Goes to hall door, calls off, upstairs)* Connie! *(She looks back significantly to* MRS. WALWORTH*)* Connie, could you come down a moment? *(She goes to* MRS. WALWORTH, *extends hand)* Now! Give it to me! She's on the stairs.

CONNIE. *(Off stage)* Yes, Annabelle.

*(*MRS. WALWORTH *quickly hands the case to* ANNABELLE, *who moves to meet* CONNIE *as she enters.)*

ANNABELLE. Connie, this is Mrs. Walworth. She was so anxious to meet you.

MRS. WALWORTH. Yes, my dear. I insisted that Annabelle call you down. Wasn't that bold of me?

CONNIE. I'm glad you did, Mrs. Walworth. I've been looking forward to meeting you.

(They shake hands.)

MRS. WALWWORTH. Oh, then you know about me? *(*MRS. WALWORTH *indicates to* CONNIE *to sit on sofa.)*

CONNIE. *(Sitting)* You were Annabelle's nurse, weren't you?

MRS. WALWORTH. No, Elizabeth's. Elizabeth and Annabelle were childhood friends you see— I'm so very happy about you and Mr. Ashton, my dear. *(She sits on sofa)* It's lovely having him happy again.

(There is a slight pause.)

Poor Elizabeth—to go so young.

*(*ANNABELLE *puts cigarette case on desk and picks up scissors.)*

So tragically. Just when everyone thought she was getting well again at last. And it was a shock to me—to think

that my gay, sweet little Elizabeth could have become
that despondent—

ANNABELLE. Connie—Mrs. Walworth—

MRS. WALWORTH. *(Rushing on, rises. Including* ANNA-
BELLE, *now)* So dreadful for Mr. Ashton—and for Annabelle. Poor Annabelle was staying with Elizabeth when
she was taken ill, you know, and she saw it happen. The
green bedroom, you know, with the balcony over the
gorge. Those frightful rocks down below. Annabelle must
have had some premonition about her friend that night.
She went to Elizabeth's room to see if she was all right—

ANNABELLE. Mrs. Walworth, really, it seems to me—

MRS. WALWORTH. It was so heroic of Annabelle.
(Moves to ANNABELLE *at desk)* Yes, it was Annabelle.
She saw Elizabeth climbing the railing—and she almost
reached her in time. Everybody in the house heard Annabelle screaming to Elizabeth— "No, Beebee, don't, Beebee, stop, Beebee—" And that was a strange thing you
know— Annabelle calling Elizabeth Beebee— She said
that in her fright she had reverted to Elizabeth's childhood nickname, Beebee. *(To* ANNABELLE*)* You hadn't
called her that in years, had you, dear? (MRS. WALWORTH
*steps to desk. Picks up cigarette case, hides it under
shawl.)*

(ANNABELLE, *defeated, moves to door.)*
Mrs. Lawson—she used to cook here. (MRS. WALWORTH
sits in chair by sofa) She says she can still hear Annabelle screaming to Elizabeth—she'll never forget it. "No,
Beebee— Beebee, no—" (MRS. WALWORTH *covers her
face with her hands.)*

CONNIE. Please, Mrs. Walworth, I know you don't
realize, but—

MRS. WALWORTH. Oh, I am sorry! *(To* ANNABELLE*)*
Please forgive me. *(To* CONNIE*)* It's true, I didn't
realize— I do get carried away. Harry always said I was
the one in the family should have been on the stage. Harry
was a baritone.

CONNIE. And your husband?

MRS. WALWORTH. Yes. For quite a while, in fact. We

came to America together twenty years ago. I've often wondered what ever came of Harry. I suppose you never ran into a Harry Walworth, did you? Nice-looking baritone? Could play small speaking parts?

CONNIE. No, I don't think so.

MRS. WALWORTH. It's just as well. Filthy temper. Harry had such a filthy temper.

(CONNIE *rises.*)

Well, my dear, I do hope you'll visit me some day soon.

CONNIE. I want to very much. Annabelle's told me about that fabulous garden of yours. I'd love to see it.

MRS. WALWORTH. Why don't you come over this Friday—when Annabelle comes?

CONNIE. I'm afraid I have a television thing that night.

MRS. WALWORTH. Really? What?

CONNIE. *(Moves to desk)* A quiz show— I'm on it to plug my last picture—and it does need to be plugged.

MRS. WALWORTH. Otherwise I'm sure you wouldn't be caught dead in the television. Such a ghastly invention! And now it is keeping you from calling on me Friday.

CONNIE. I'll come as soon as I can, I promise. Joe and I will walk over this afternoon.

MRS. WALWORTH. Joe? Who may I ask is Joe? Not that he isn't welcome.

CONNIE. Nobody important. Just a little old dog of mine. *(She glances around room)* He's around here some place. *(To* ANNABELLE*)* Have you seen him, Annabelle?

ANNABELLE. He's with the children, I think.

CONNIE. I'll take a look. I'll see you again soon, Mrs. Walworth. *(She exits to terrace.)*

MRS. WALWORTH. Yes, indeed. *(Looking after* CONNIE*)* Vital. Good peasant stock, I should imagine. But not half Elizabeth's class though. Well, my dear, it's no effort to be pleasant is it? *(Puts cigarette case into purse)* We won't quarrel any more. It wasn't really a quarrel though, was it. Just a misunderstanding.

ANNABELLE. *(Moves to* MRS. WALWORTH *with scissors)* I find you very amusing, Mrs. Walworth. That scene with

Connie. You should have been an actress—but I warn you—don't try it again.

RICKY. *(Enters from hall)* Where's Connie? I thought I heard her in here.

ANNABELLE. *(Goes to desk, puts scissors on it)* She's gone out to look for Joe. Why did you want her?

RICKY. I was supposed to tell Dad that she was ready to come home and—

ANNABELLE. Yes, and you forgot, didn't you?

RICKY. Is she mad?

ANNABELLE. Ricky, say hello to Mrs. Walworth.

RICKY. Hello, Mrs. Walworth.

MRS. WALWORTH. That's a good boy. *(Rises, picks up drink, sits on sofa.)*

ANNABELLE. *(To* RICKY) You can hardly expect Connie to be pleased, Ricky. Such a long hike on a hot day.

RICKY. *(Stricken)* Did she have to *walk?*

ANNABELLE. All the way, yes.

RICKY. I better tell her I'm sorry— *(He starts towards terrace.)*

ANNABELLE. Ricky!

RICKY. *(Turns back)* Yes, Miss Annabelle?

ANNABELLE. The damage has already been done and I'm afraid it won't make Connie any less annoyed with you. I shouldn't bother her if I were you.

RICKY. *(Sullen)* All right, I won't apologize. That's all I've been doing ever since she got here anyway—apologizing. *(Stands facing her.)*

ANNABELLE. *(With a great sigh)* I know it's difficult for you. But you must realize, my dear, I've tried often enough to explain it to you— Connie isn't used to children. She's an actress. Actresses aren't like other mothers. You must learn to be quiet, for instance. You can't go screaming about the house in the morning like wild Indians any more, you and Janie.

RICKY. We've got to have *some* fun—

ANNABELLE. In a different way, Ricky. Now that Connie's here, things will naturally have to be a little different.

RICKY. *(Resentfully)* I won't move. When I'm in the

house, I'll whisper. She can sleep all day if she wants to. I'll pretend I'm dead.

ANNABELLE. Now, now—you know it would hurt Connie to hear you say that.

RICKY. Well— *(He decides to skip it)* Can I go work on my boat now?

ANNABELLE. I'm afraid you're not to work on your boat any more today. That might help you to control your feelings—to be a little more understanding about Connie and a great deal less rude.

RICKY. But I've got to work on my boat! I'll never get it finished!

ANNABELLE. I'm sorry.

RICKY. *(Moving away)* I can't do anything any more— Not with her here.

ANNABELLE. *(Reaches out and takes his arm and turns him around to her)* Be patient—it will be much better in a little while, I promise you.

RICKY. No, it won't! When you go back to London next week, it'll be worse! A lot worse!

ANNABELLE. Please, darling—

RICKY. *(Pulling away from* ANNABELLE*)* I don't care! Everything was fine until she came— I don't care. *(He runs out to hall.)*

ANNABELLE. Ricky!

   (He is gone.)

Oh, dear, he is a problem—

MRS. WALWORTH. You're leaving for London next week? You'd led me to believe it wouldn't be nearly so soon.

ANNABELLE. Did I?

MRS. WALWORTH. I was under the impression that we had plenty of time to make our arrangements. We do have arrangements to make, you know.

ANNABELLE. *(Rises)* I'm so sorry you don't have time for another drink before you go.

MRS. WALWORTH. Now don't be unfriendly. What will you do in London?

   *(ANNABELLE *closes hall door.)*

Oh, your income is enough to manage my forty a week. I've no fears about that. But in order to live as you've become accustomed to here, you'll need some sort of job to earn a bit extra.

ANNABELLE. *(Comes down to* MRS. WALWORTH*)* I can hardly believe you're seriously worried about my comfort.

MRS. WALWORTH. Interested, not worried. I couldn't really worry about anyone as resourceful as you are, my dear.

ANNABELLE. Thank you so much.

MRS. WALWORTH. You are resourceful, Annabelle! No one would think it to look at you. You don't look at all the type to organize and manage—and push people off balconies, do you, dear?

ANNABELLE. If anyone heard you say that, it would end your forty a week, you know.

MRS. WALWORTH. Yes, I do know that. Really, I am careful. *(She takes a drink.)*

ANNABELLE. I do wish you'd stop drinking so much.

MRS. WALWORTH. It isn't so much. It doesn't seem nearly enough. But I will try. *(She takes another drink.)*

ANNABELLE. At least try to confine it to the privacy of your charming cottage. Pub crawling is such a disreputable habit. *(She goes to desk.)*

MRS. WALWORTH. *(Putting drink on coffee table)* Has Mr. Ashton given you a going-away present yet? A handsome sum, perhaps?

ANNABELLE. No.

MRS. WALWORTH. But he will, of course. And the moment he does, I shall expect you to remember me.

ANNABELLE. Charles' present to me is a first class passage on the *Queen Mary.*

MRS. WALWORTH. *(Squawking with laughter)* Absolutely the last thing in the world you wanted! But I've no idea why I'm laughing. *(She rises)* That cuts my throat a bit, you know. *(She steps toward* ANNABELLE*)* Do you think you might borrow— Oh, say, ten thousand dollars from Mr. Ashton? For me?

ANNABELLE. No, I don't think so.

MRS. WALWORTH. We could call our account settled then. It's been so degrading for you to come trotting to me every Friday with your two little twenty dollar bills.

ANNABELLE. You're being so very thoughtful, Mrs. Walworth. How unlike you.

MRS. WALWORTH. It's not possible for you to send money from England, you know. The only solution is for you to speak to Mr. Ashton. Ten thousand dollars—would mean nothing to him.

ANNABELLE. We'll discuss it some other time. At your place.

MRS. WALWORTH. It wouldn't be asking much. It isn't as though you'd been on the payroll, my dear. Really, how could he be so ungrateful? Why, you could even ask a litle more— Eleven thousand. Perhaps even eleven-five. *(Sitting Center)* I won't let you leave for London without settling up with me.

ANNABELLE. *(Slowly goes to* MRS. WALWORTH, *then speaks)* My dear Mrs. Walworth. I'm not going back to London.

MRS. WALWORTH. Not? Oh, but I'm afraid you must. There's no need for you any more, not with the movie actress here.

ANNABELLE. *(Crossing to Left of Center chair)* The movie actress won't be here for long.

MRS. WALWORTH. Oh, perhaps I see. You're trying to drive her away. That's why you've turned the boy against her. You mean to break up the marriage.

ANNABELLE. No, I couldn't do that. I don't believe that could be done. It will have to be something else. Something more than that.

(MRS. WALWORTH *gasps, shocked.* MILDRED *raps on the door.* ANNABELLE *moves away from* MRS. WAL- WORTH *as* MILDRED *enters.)*

MILDRED. It's the photographer from the paper, and two of the ladies.

ANNABELLE. Oh, yes. *(Goes to desk and gets list.)*

MILDRED. They're on the front terrace, Miss Annabelle.

ANNABELLE. I'll be right out.

MILDRED. Yes ma'am. (MILDRED *exits through hall.*)

ANNABELLE. *(Goes to* MRS. WALWORTH) Mrs. Walworth, you must excuse me. The picture for the Visiting Nurses' Auction, you know. Now do run along home, dear. *(She touches* MRS. WALWORTH *on the arm)* Do be charming. *(She exits through hall door.)*

(MRS. WALWORTH *sits, stunned, then her head turns slowly as she hears* CONNIE *beyond the terrace.)*

CONNIE. *(Off)* Here, Joe! Here, Joe, boy! Here, baby!

CURTAIN

ACT ONE

SCENE II

The library.

Half an hour later.

As the Curtain rises, CHARLES *is sitting on sofa, reading. VOICES are heard off on terrace.* CONNIE *enters through terrace doors.*

CHARLES. *(As she enters)* Get your picture taken?

CONNIE. Got my picture taken, it was fun. *(She sits on sofa.)*

CHARLES. Of course it was fun. You were the star.

CONNIE. I'd say Annabelle and I co-starred. She's a big wheel in the Visiting Nurses. Charles, she's leaving next week?

CHARLES. Friday. The *Queen Mary.*

CONNIE. It's definite then?

(CHARLES *nods.*)

I'm glad she's going. Oh, I know how wonderful she's been, all she's done for the children, but I can't help it. I wish she were leaving sooner. Is that an awful thing to say?

CHARLES. Of course not. I know exactly how you feel—

CONNIE. I feel as though I were a guest here—and not a very welcome one. I think Ricky and I could get together once Annabelle's gone—

CHARLES. It's only another week—

CONNIE. It's going to be a long week!

CHARLES. Maybe I could get the *Queen Mary* to sail a couple of days earlier.

CONNIE. *(Rises)* Oh, don't pay any attention to me. Maybe I'm just passing the buck because I haven't made the grade with Ricky. But I will—

CHARLES. All you need is a little time, that's all.

CONNIE. I've always got along with kids. We like each other, kids and I.

CHARLES. *(Rises)* Of course you do. *(He kisses her as VOICES are again heard off on terace.)*

CONNIE. *(Breaking kiss)* Darling, don't get involved. Run. I'll be along in a minute.

CHARLES. All right. I'll get the car out. (CHARLES *rises and starts for terrace.)*

    (MRS. WALWORTH *enters from terrace and meets* CHARLES.)

Mrs. Walworth! How are you?

MRS. WALWORTH. *(Extending hand to* CHARLES, *who shakes it)* Splendid. Congratulations, Mr. Ashton. I'm sure you'll be very happy, you and Connie.

CHARLES. Thank you.

MRS. WALWORTH. What a lovely tie clasp you have there!

CHARLES. Thank you very much.

MRS. WALWORTH. Perfectly lovely. Take care of it.

(CHARLES *exits to terrace, as* RICKY *enters from hall. He has a gin and tonic.)*

MRS. WALWORTH. *(Taking drink from him)* You're a dear boy. What took you so long? *(She takes a sip.)*

RICKY. I made it myself. Is it all right?

MRS. WALWORTH. Very nice. I hope you do your lessons half as well.

ANNABELLE. *(Entering through terrace doors)* Connie, you inspired our photographer. He was thrilled. Thanks so much for posing with us.

CONNIE. I enjoyed it.

ANNABELLE. I imagine that dress photographs beautifully. You must take it with you on Saturday. *(She sits, turns to* MRS. WALWORTH*)* Charles and Connie are invited for the week-end.

RICKY. *(To* CONNIE*)* You're going away on Saturday?

CONNIE. Yes, Ricky, why?

RICKY. The Carnival's this week—the Kiwanis carnival. My father always takes us on Saturday.

ANNABELLE. We'll take you another day.

RICKY. But the Death Defying Leap is only on Saturday. I can't miss that!

CONNIE. I didn't know that, Ricky. Maybe we could arrange to—

ANNABELLE. Sweetie, this could be terribly important. Mr. Jackson could be one of your father's biggest clients. You do understand, don't you? Mr. Jackson wants to see your father's plans for his new building—and he wants to meet Connie.

RICKY. On Saturday?

ANNABELLE. Yes, dear. On Saturday.

RICKY. *(Turning away)* Gee, I always see the Death Defying Leap— It's a habit I have— *(He sits in front desk chair.)*

ANNABELLE. Now, now, Ricky.

(JANIE *enters from Right wearing* CONNIE'S *green shawl, white gloves, and carrying her green purse.)* Well, look at us! Aren't we stunning?

JANIE. Thank you, Miss Annabelle. You should see me in Connie's mink coat. She's going to let me wear it when I get big enough, aren't you?

CONNIE. *(Taking gloves from* JANIE*)* It's yours for the Junior Prom, Janie, that's a deal.

ANNABELLE. Mrs. Walworth, Connie's mink—it's fabulous. *(To* CONNIE*)* You must be very proud of it.

CONNIE. *(Taking shawl)* Frankly, I am proud of it. It's the story of my life. I earned it all by my little self—by getting up early in the morning, not staying out late at night. ·

(Auomobile HORN blows twice.)

Oh, Janie, is Joe upstairs?

JANIE. No.

CONNIE. Did you look under my bed? *(Putting on gloves.)* `

JANIE. *(Nodding)* Every place. He isn't up there, I'm sure.

CONNIE. Where could that little mutt be? *(Gets purse from* JANIE*)* He might have wandered off some place—

ANNABELLE. He's around some place. The children will find him.

JANIE. I'll look outside for him. *(She starts running toward terrace)* 'Bye, have a good time. *(She exits.)*

CONNIE. Thank you, Janie.

ANNABELLE. Ricky, you go help Janie look for Joe.

RICKY. Okay! *(He rises and starts out after* JANIE.*)*

ANNABELLE. *(Halting* RICKY*)* And what do you say?

RICKY. *(Begrudgingly)* Good-bye. Have a good time. *(He exits.)*

ANNABELLE. *(Shaking her head, laughs)* Yes, Connie, good-bye, have a good time.

CONNIE. *(Starts for terrace)* Since Ricky insists I will. *(Turns back)* Mrs. Walworth, I *am* coming over to see you.

MRS. WALWORTH. *(Rising)* Soon, I hope.

CONNIE. *(Going)* Very soon. Good-bye, we won't be late.

ANNABELLE. Good-bye, Connie.

*(*CONNIE *exits.* MRS. WALWORTH *checks that* CONNIE *has gone, goes to hall door, closes it, and then comes back to* ANNABELLE, *who is sitting on sofa.)*

MRS. WALWORTH. I absolutely forbid you even to consider it.

ANNABELLE. *(Rising)* I suppose it was too much to hope you'd go home. *(She goes to desk.)*

MRS. WALWORTH. I know how much you love him. You'd stop at nothing to get him back. *(She goes to* ANNABELLE*)* But you mustn't do it. You mustn't!

ANNABELLE. If there were a less difficult way to get rid of her, I'd be very happy.

MRS. WALWORTH. I know how you must loathe her, but you won't listen to me.

ANNABELLE. I don't loathe her at all. I find her rather charming. *(Almost to herself)* But when someone takes what belongs to you—you do what is necessary to get it back.

MRS. WALWORTH. I know—you've decided he's yours —just as you did with Little Lucinda's doll. You remember kidnapping Lucinda's doll and hiding it away, don't you? You still don't think that was naughty of you, do you? You still don't think it was wrong about Elizabeth, do you? Naughty, right and wrong—such silly words, aren't they?

ANNABELLE. *(Goes to sofa)* Coming from you, dear, they're hilarious! *(Sits.)*

MRS. WALWORTH. What do you mean by that?

ANNABELLE. I mean that to me blackmailing is a particularly degrading occupation.

MRS. WALWORTH. One must make a living. It's hardly fair of you to criticize me for being too proud to go on relief.

ANNABELLE. Finish your drink and run along. I do wish you would. You bore me.

MRS. WALWORTH. You might have a little consideration for me. *(She sits in chair by sofa)* Something might go wrong and with you in prison—there goes my forty a week!

ANNABELLE. Nothing shall go wrong. I hope you've made no plans for Friday—this Friday.

MRS. WALWORTH. You aren't thinking of—you're not expecting to go about it this Friday!

ANNABELLE. Yes, it has to be then. Friday I shall expect you to spend the afternoon in your cottage—alone. Are your gladiolas in bloom?

MRS. WALWORTH. My gladiolas!

ANNABELLE. I shall need a rather large bouquet. You must bring them over here about noon on Friday. You'll hide them behind the old carriage house. Be very careful that no one sees you.

MRS. WALWORTH. Incredible! You even hoped I would become an active accomplice!

ANNABELLE. You will be running no risk whatsoever. *(Pauses, then rises and goes to terrace doors)* Ricky! Oh, Ricky, dear, would you come in please, for a minute? *(She comes back to desk.)*

(RICK enters through terrace doors.)
Ricky, did you find Joe?
(He shakes his head.)
Is Janie still looking for him?

RICKY. Yes. Do I have to? Can't I work on my boat?

ANNABELLE. *(Going to vault. Opens louvered doors)* Ricky, dear, would you help me? I want to use the vault for storage. Would you open it for me?

RICKY. *(Running to vault)* Gee, thanks!

(As he goes to vault, ANNABELLE moves back to desk. MRS. WALWORTH, aware that ANNABELLE is up to something, watches RICKY.)

ANNABELLE. Having trouble, dear?

RICKY. *(Working combination)* No, I've got it— *(He swings open the steel door)* There!

ANNABELLE. Good boy. I suppose it does need a good cleanout, doesn't it?

RICKY. I don't know— *(He steps into vault to see.)*
(A pause.)
Miss Annabelle! Come here, quick!!

ANNABELLE. *(Hurrying to vault)* What is it, dear?

RICKY. *(Crying. Still inside vault)* It's Joe!

ANNABELLE. Oh, Ricky, no— *(She swings* RICKY *away from vault)* Don't look, dear. He's dead!

(MRS. WALWORTH *turns front.)*

RICKY. How did it happen? How did Joe get in there?

ANNABELLE. *(Stepping to* RICKY, *puts her arm around him)* You poor child. You don't even realize what you've done, do you?

RICKY. What?

ANNABELLE. *(Hugging* RICKY *to her)* Ricky, Ricky, Ricky—you were a naughty boy. You opened the vault— you left it open for quite a while. Little Joe crawled in— perhaps he went to sleep, I don't know— But when you closed the door—

(MRS. WALWORTH *sits on sofa.)*

RICKY. You told me to!

ANNABELLE. Yes, and when you did, little Joe couldn't breathe. Nobody could hear him barking—poor little thing. He suffocated— *(She holds him off at arms' length)* because you were a naughty boy and played with the vault. You did it, Ricky.

RICKY. No, no!! I didn't see him go in!

ANNABELLE. Of course you didn't see him go in! You didn't do it intentionally. It was an accident. But you did do it.

RICKY. What will happen? What will they do to me?

ANNABELLE. *(Releasing* RICKY *and going to chair by coffee table)* I don't know. I don't know what they'll do —but they'll be very, very angry. It was a naughty thing you did.

RICKY. But I didn't mean to do it.

ANNABELLE. Do you think they'll believe that? You haven't been very nice to Connie, you don't like her. Your father knows that. *(Sitting in arm of chair)* I'm afraid he may think you did it on purpose.

RICKY. *(Going to her, taking her hand)* Oh, no, it was an accident! You'll tell them that, won't you, Miss Annabelle?

ANNABELLE. *(Holding both his hands)* Will that do any good, dear? But I'll help you, Ricky. I'll think of something. What can I do? What ever can I do? I know. We won't tell them little Joe got caught in the vault, because then they'd know you did it. I have it! I'll put him out on the lawn—perhaps they'll think he was hit by a car. Something like that.

RICKY. Yes!

ANNABELLE. All right, dear. Go up to your room now. *(She smoothes his hair)* You're hot and upset. You must rest a little. Go up and lie down for a while. Everything will be all right, I promise.

RICKY. Yes, Miss Annabelle. *(Sobbing, he runs out Right.)*

(There is a pause. ANNABELLE slowly turns to MRS. WALWORTH. ANNABELLE smiles, pleased with herself. Then she rises, goes up to vault and closes and locks the steel door. She closes the louvered doors. She turns back to MRS. WALWORTH, waits.)

MRS. WALWORTH. *(Takes cigarette case from purse. Polishing fingerprints from it)* Of course, my dear, I shall have to raise my rates. Double at least I should think. That would be eighty dollars the week. *(She puts case on coffee table and sits.)*

ANNABELLE. *(Opens the hall doors. Then she goes to the bell pull. Pulls bell pull)* I should like some tea— *(She joins MRS. WALWORTH)* A nice cup of tea—

CURTAIN

ACT TWO

Scene I

The library.

The following Friday, shortly before noon.

At rise the stage is empty. ANNABELLE *enters quickly from Right, conscious that someone is approaching from terrace. She goes directly to desk, takes a pair of scissors from her pocket and sits above desk. She is about to put the scissors in sheath when she notices a thread caught in the blades. She disentangles it, puts the scissors in sheath, and puts the sheath in the top drawer and busies herself with papers on desk as* CONNIE *enters from terrace.*

ANNABELLE. Connie, dear! Where's Janie? Didn't she go walking with you?

CONNIE. Yes—she's watching Ricky work on his boat.

ANNABELLE. *(Picking up newspaper)* Come see this! On the front page just as they promised. I'm so pleased!

CONNIE. *(Takes paper)* Well—look at me! I owe the Visiting Nurses an apology—and a large contribution.

ANNABELLE. It's a beautiful picture of you—and thank you so much. Connie, Doctor Lindstrum phoned while you were out.

CONNIE. Oh, yes.

ANNABELLE. I hope you didn't mind my sending Joe to the vet's?

CONNIE. No, of course not. I want to know what happened.

ANNABELLE. Well, he says there are no broken bones, no marks at all. He couldn't have been hit by a car or killed in a fight with another dog. He asked me if there was any likelihood of his being poisoned. I told him we'd considered that and we couldn't believe it possible. Anyway, he's going to perform an autopsy. I said it was all right. I hope you agree.

CONNIE. *(Turning away)* Yes— *(She goes to sofa)* It's a beautiful day, isn't it?

ANNABELLE. Yes, Connie, dear. You're quite right.

(CONNIE *sits on sofa with newspaper.*) Are you planning on taking your green dress to Pawling on Saturday?

CONNIE. I thought I would.

ANNABELLE. Fine. I'll have it pressed and that will be done and out of the way. *(She pulls bell pull.)*

CONNIE. *(Laughs but annoyed)* Annabelle, I can take care of my own clothes! I can ask Mildred to press my dress.

ANNABELLE. *(Back at desk)* I enjoy it. I hope Charles won't be later than he thought. I've ordered an early lunch.

MILDRED. *(Enters from hall)* Yes, Ma'am?

ANNABELLE. Mildred, will you press Mrs. Ashton's green dress—

CONNIE. Don't bother, Mildred. It's silly to press it, then pack it—

ANNABELLE. Mildred packs beautifully. There won't be a wrinkle in it. *(To MILDRED)* I've laid it out on Mrs. Ashton's bed.

(MILDRED *hesitates.*)

CONNIE. Very well, Mildred.

MILDRED. Yes, Ma'am. *(She exits to hall.)*

ANNABELLE. Do you still intend to take the four-eighteen?

CONNIE. The four-eighteen, yes.

ANNABELLE. Then you will have time for some shopping—and I wanted to remind you—do look at those wonderful cashmeres at Saks. You'll find I'm not being a bit over-enthusiastic about them.

CONNIE. I don't know about shopping— I thought I'd stop in and see Betsy McLane.

ANNABELLE. *(Casually)* Oh, really? I gathered you were so looking forward to an hour's shopping.

CONNIE. No, I thought I'd have Betsy calm me down about this television thing.

ANNABELLE. Connie! You're not nervous about it!

CONNIE. Well, let's say I'm uneasy. I'd like Betsy to brief me. She's an old hand at quiz shows.

ANNABELLE. Does she know you're coming, dear? Is she expecting you?

CONNIE. No, and I won't bother calling her. I'll just drop in. She'll be home resting for her performance tonight.

(ANNABELLE *turns back to desk as* MILDRED *enters from hall. She carries the green dress; she is upset.)*

MILDRED. *(Urgently)* Miss Annabelle—

ANNABELLE. Mildred, for Heaven's sake, what is it?

MILDRED. Something terrible—

CONNIE. What is it? The children!

MILDRED. Oh, no, Mrs. Ashton! It's this dress, your dress—

CONNIE. *(Relieved)* Mildred! Oh, if it's only my dress—

MILDRED. Mrs. Ashton—look! *(She holds it up)* It's been ruined! It's in shreds!

CONNIE. What happened to it?

MILDRED. It wasn't an accident, it was on purpose. Look! It's been cut—slashed with a knife or something.

CONNIE. Slashed with a knife—but who—

(A pause.)

ANNABELLE. What on earth—

MILDRED. *(Reluctantly)* Ricky—it must have been Ricky—

(CHARLES *enters from terrace. He carries a roll of blueprints, puts them on desk.)*

CONNIE. No, he wouldn't— Ricky couldn't do a thing like that!

CHARLES. Ricky couldn't do a thing like what? What's going on?

ANNABELLE. Connie's dress, Charles—show it to him, Mildred.

MILDRED. *(Holds up dress)* It's all cut—ruined—

CHARLES. *(Takes dress, looks at it)* Ricky couldn't have done that.

CONNIE. No!

MILDRED. It must have been him, Mr. Ashton.

CHARLES. Why should he? Where was the dress?

ANNABELLE. On Connie's bed. I laid it out just after Connie and Janie went for a walk. That was about eleven.

CHARLES. Has Ricky been upstairs since then

ANNABELLE. He might have been, I don't know.

CHARLES. Mildred, do you know?

MILDRED. Yes, he was. He didn't go down to his boat till a little while ago.

ANNABELLE. *(Quietly, as though she hated saying it)* Yes, Mildred's right, I'm afraid. I remember—Ricky was upstairs when I laid out the dress.

CHARLES. Mildred, will you ask Ricky to come here?
(She hesitates.)
Just say that I want to see him.

MILDRED. Yes, sir. *(Goes out to terrace.)*

CONNIE. *(Miserably)* The poor kid—darling, he couldn't have realized—

ANNABELLE. Yes, Charles, let's not exaggerate this.

CHARLES. *(Impatiently)* I'm not exaggerating anything! I'm not going to horsewhip the kid— I'm going to *talk* to him.

ANNABELLE. But listen to me, please. You see, I think I know exactly why Ricky did this. He wanted to go to the carnival tomorrow—you know that. He had his heart set on seeing the Death Defying Leap. Now don't you see? He must have thought that by ruining Connie's dress it would prevent you from going to Pawling tomorrow. And you'd take him to the carnival instead.

CONNIE. I never realized that it meant so much to him! Charles, how stupid of us! We could have gone to Pawling later—

CHARLES. Sure we could. But at the moment that isn't the point. When a nine-year-old boy can take a knife and do what he did! Because he wants to go to a carnival—

MILDRED. *(Enters from terrace)* Here he is, Mr. Ashton.

CHARLES. Thank you, Mildred.

MILDRED. *(Calls out to terrace)* Come on in, Ricky. *(She exits to hall.)*

(RICKY *enters slowly from terrace. He is uncertain, a little frightened. He comes to the Center of the room, though, and stands directly in front of* CHARLES. *He looks at him quizzically.)*

CHARLES. Do you know why I wanted to see you, Ricky?

RICKY. No. Mildred just said you did.

CHARLES. You seem—a little worried.

RICKY. Mildred said you wanted to see me this minute. When she says "this minute" I know it's nothing good.

CHARLES. Look, Rick, it isn't good. *(Holds up dress)* This is Connie's dress. You see what happened to it?

RICKY. It's all torn.

CHARLES. It was slashed with a knife.

RICKY. *(Knows he's going to be blamed for it. He becomes tense, frightened)* I didn't do anything!

CHARLES. Ricky, you know Connie was going to wear that dress tomorrow, didn't you? And you want to go to the carnival tomorrow instead of today—

RICKY. I didn't tear her dress!

CHARLES. No one else could have done it—

RICKY. I didn't! I didn't go near her old dress!

CHARLES. *(Drops dress on desk. Puts arm around* RICKY's *shoulder)* Ricky, sometimes people want things so badly—they go about getting them in the wrong way. They get mad and mixed up and they do things—things they'd give their right arm not to have done, but it's too late. Then the only thing they can do is to tell the truth and say they're sorry—

RICKY. But I'm not sorry! I didn't do it—

CHARLES. We know you did— *(Turns away from* RICKY) I'm going to have to punish you.

RICKY. Go ahead, punish me. I don't care— How are you going to punish me? Stay in my room? I can't work on my boat.

CHARLES. Nothing that easy. I'm sorry. Something more than that.

RICKY. *(Quietly, bitterly)* I didn't do it. I didn't touch her—

CHARLES. Go to your room, Ricky.

RICKY. I never even saw—

CHARLES. Go to your room!

RICKY. Yes, sir! *(He runs out Right.)*

CHARLES. *(Going to* CONNIE) Darling, Ricky didn't do this to you—he doesn't feel that way about you—

CONNIE. I hope not—I hope not—

CHARLES. It was his way of getting to see the Death Defying Leap tomorrow—

ANNABELLE. Charles, perhaps he shouldn't go to the carnival at all.

CHARLES. Maybe, you're right.

CONNIE. Darling—

CHARLES. He's got to be punished. Maybe this is what he needs, maybe we've been too lenient with him.

JANIE. *(Enters from Right)* What's wrong with Ricky? He won't talk to me, he slammed the door.

ANNABELLE. He's been a naughty boy, dear—never mind—

JANIE. What did he do?

CHARLES. Don't worry about it, Janie.

ANNABELLE. You worry about lunch. It's almost ready. Off you go!

JANIE. *(Going to hall door)* What are we having?

ANNABELLE. Wait and be surprised. Oh, Charles, Connie's taking the four-eighteen and I'll be getting back from Mrs. Walworth's by then. Yes, that will be all right.

CHARLES. What will be all right?

ANNABELLE. I don't want Ricky to be left alone.

CONNIE. Alone?

ANNABELLE. Yes, you see, I've given the servants the afternoon off. So they can go to the carnival, too. There'll be no one here this afternoon but you and Ricky. Have a nice lunch, my dears.

JANIE. *(In hall doorway)* Come on, Daddy—

(JANIE *takes* CHARLES' *hand and they exit.)*

ANNABELLE. *(Halting* CONNIE *as she starts to follow* CHARLES) Oh, Connie. It will be all right— I'm sure—

CONNIE. *(Grimly, but smiling)* Thank you, Annabelle. *(She exits.)*

(ANNABELE *goes to desk, picks up dress. Highly satisfied with her progress, smiling, she starts for door Right.* MRS. WALWORTH *appears in terrace door. She is carrying a large bunch of purple gladiolas.)*

MRS. WALWORTH. *(Whispering hoarsely)* My dear!

ANNABELLE. *(Startled, whirls toward her, throwing dress onto chair)* What are you doing here?

MRS. WALWORTH. *(Entering)* Annabelle, my dear—

ANNABELLE. *(Going to her)* Does anyone know you've come? Did anyone see you?

MRS. WALWORTH. Not a soul, but it doesn't matter. I've changed my mind.

(ANNABELLE *quickly goes to hall door and closes it.)*

(MRS. WALWORTH *moves into Center of room)* Yes, I have. You're not to go through with it.

ANNABELLE. *(Facing her)* Sit down—be quiet, let me think! *(She snatches the gladiolas from* MRS. WALWORTH) The glads are all that matter. I can explain your being here, but if anyone saw the glads—you're positive no one saw you?

MRS. WALWORTH. Quite. There's no one at all about. But you needn't concern yourself—

ANNABELLE. Please be quiet—just be quiet! (ANNA-BELLE *goes to cupboard with glads. She opens top cupboard, puts glads in it, closes it, locks it and puts key in her pocket. She goes back to* MRS. WALWORTH) You've been drinking, haven't you?

MRS. WALWORTH. A drop to steady my nerves.

ANNABELLE. More than a drop. I can see that. Much more than a drop. On the day I needed you most.

MRS. WALWORTH. You don't listen. I've decided not to let you do it.

ANNABELLE. As though you could stop me!

MRS. WALWORTH. Oh, I can stop you easily enough. *(Takes letter from purse and waves it in front of* ANNA-BELLE) With our little Lucinda's help. *(She continues holding letter toward* ANNABELLE.)

ANNABELLE. *(Controls herself, gently, reasoningly)* Mrs. Walworth, has something happened? What's made you change your mind? I assure you, there's no need at all to be nervous.

MRS. WALWORTH. *(Returns letter to purse)* Something might go wrong.

ANNABELLE. Everything is going splendidly. I can't imagine what is upsetting you.

MRS. WALWORTH. I don't know—so many things—

ANNABELLE. *(Seating* MRS. WALWORTH *on sofa, sits beside her)* If you could be more definite?

MRS. WALWORTH. Well—the vault. Yes, the vault.

ANNABELLE. Now, just what about the vault?

MRS. WALWORTH. The dog—did it really suffocate? It might have killed itself somehow trying to get out.

ANNABELLE. The vault is quite air-tight. Of course, the poor little dog was in a frenzy. It took about an hour for the dog. It will take two for her.

MRS. WALWORTH. You seem so certain of that.

ANNABELLE. Oh, yes, I made certain of it. It was rather a frightening experience, I must say.

MRS. WALWORTH. You put yourself in the vault?

ANNABELLE. Yes! The first hour and a half was most uncomfortable. Then it began to get oppressive. In about

an hour and three-quarters, I was gasping and I almost
blacked out. Another few minutes would have surely
done me in. So you see, I am quite certain. Two hours.

MRS. WALWORTH. She's a bit younger and quicker than
you—

ANNABELLE. Don't let that concern you. They're all
at lunch now. Everyone will be gone by three—except the
two of them, of course. By three-thirty— *(She rises)* —I
should have her in there. No one will be getting back
much before half-past five, and by that time—two hours
—that will have done it.

MRS. WALWORTH. I don't know. That seems to be cutting it rather close to me.

ANNABELLE. *(Facing* MRS. WALWORTH) No, actually,
it will all be over by five-thirty. But even then she won't
be missed till after eight. That's when she's due at the
television studio. I expect the television people will phone
a bit after eight. And it might take hours—before anyone
realizes where she is.

MRS. WALWORTH. Aren't you worried that she may not
cooperate and go into the vault?

ANNABELLE. Dear, please give me credit for a little
intelligence. She'll go into the vault.

MRS. WALWORTH. Yes, but once you've slammed the
door and locked it—well, it occurs to me that if I were in
her shoes, I'd do a great deal of screaming.

ANNABELLE. You would, yes, but she won't. *(Moving
to desk)* She'll realize it's quite useless—nobody would
hear her. She'll keep her head.

MRS. WALWORTH. But she just might scream, and
somebody might hear her.

ANNABELLE. *(Turns back to* MRS. WALWORTH) Did
you hear the dog barking? You were here in the room
at the time. Did you hear the dog?

MRS. WALWORTH. No.

ANNABELLE. There you are!

MRS. WALWORTH. How do I know it was barking?

ANNABELLE. What, my dear?

MRS. WALWORTH. If I couldn't hear it bark, how could I possibly know if it was barking or not?

ANNABELLE. I do wish you wouldn't drink.

MRS. WALWORTH. Did you hear it bark?

ANNABELLE. No, of course not!

MRS. WALWORTH. Well!

ANNABELLE. *(Goes to vault, throws open louvered doors)* Come here! Come and look at the thickness of the door and walls.

> *(She works combination as* MRS. WALWORTH *joins her.)*

(ANNABELLE *throws open the steel door)* There you are!

MRS. WALWORTH. *(Peering into vault)* Gloomy, isn't it! And so small! Not the least bit inviting.

ANNABELLE. No, but if you like I'll go in and close the door and scream my head off. You won't hear a sound.

MRS. WALWORTH. Now, don't be silly, Annabelle. I couldn't possibly trust you. I'm sure you wouldn't bother to open your mouth.

ANNABELLE. I'd promise.

MRS. WALWORTH. No. So long as I lived I'd never know if you had screamed or not.

ANNABELLE. Very well. You go in, and you scream.

MRS. WALWORTH. *(Looks at* ANNABELLE *a moment, starts into vault, then reconsiders and moves quickly away)* No. No, really, let's not even consider that.

ANNABELLE. *(Closes vault door)* At the moment, you're completely indispensable to me.

MRS. WALWORTH. Why, yes, I am, aren't I? Your alibi. Yes, you must keep me safe and sound, mustn't you? Come to think of it, I haven't enjoyed such a sense of security in your presence for quite some time. Still— *(She glances at vault and then moves to desk)* I much prefer being on this side of that door.

ANNABELLE. *(Closing outer doors of vault)* Then you'll just have to take my word for it. (ANNABELLE *goes to* MRS. WALWORTH) Now are you quite happy about everything?

MRS. WALWORTH. I'm encouraged—yes, you've been

most encouraging. But I should like to think a little—

ANNABELLE. I'm afraid there's hardly time for that. You know, I *have* agreed that it would mean eighty a week for you, and perhaps a bit more.

MRS. WALWORTH. I must say that is tempting—

(CONNIE *is heard in the hall.* ANNABELLE *goes to desk and* MRS. WALWORTH *gets purse from sofa, as* CONNIE *enters.)*

ANNABELLE. Did you have a nice lunch, Connie?

CONNIE. Very nice. Hello, Mrs. Walworth.

MRS. WALWORTH. My dear, how are you?

(CONNIE *goes to coffee table for a cigarette.)*

ANNABELLE. Mrs. Walworth is just leaving. She was in the neighborhood and stopped in to make sure I was coming for tea this afternoon.

MRS. WALWORTH. And I'm so glad you can, Annabelle. Come as early as you can— I do get so lonely.

ANNABELLE. *(Sitting behind desk)* You poor thing! I'll be there shortly after three.

MRS. WALWORTH. *(Turns and looks at* CONNIE*)* I don't believe I've told you—and I do want you to know. I've enjoyed your pictures so much, so very much. *(She turns front, looks at* ANNABELLE, *then back to* CONNIE*)* Goodbye, my dear. *(She exits to terrace.)*

CURTAIN

ACT TWO

SCENE II

The library.

Later the same afternoon.

At rise CHARLES *is standing in the terrace doorway.*

ANNABELLE *enters from Right. She has changed from her house dress to tweeds and walking shoes.*

CHARLES. *(Calling)* Janie! Janie—hurry up, baby!

ANNABELLE. Oh, you've found her?

CHARLES. *(Turning to her)* Yes, I did.

ANNABELLE. Good. I almost wish I were going with you.

CHARLES. You're invited.

ANNABELLE. No, Mrs. Walworth is expecting me. I mustn't disappoint her—and then I've promised Connie I'd bring her back some gladiolas.

JANIE. *(Runs in from terrace)* Is it time to go?

CHARLES. It's time for you to get ready to go. Connie's waiting to get you started.

JANIE. I wish Ricky was going. Can't he, please?

CHARLES. No, baby.

JANIE. It'd be more fun.

CHARLES. You and I will have fun. *(Slaps her on her bottom; starts her toward door Right)* On your horse, sweetheart.

ANNABELLE. *(Stopping JANIE)* You'll have a lovely time, Janie. It's a gorgeous afternoon and the carnival's always so very gay. Charles, why don't you take some color pictures?

JANIE. Yes, Daddy! Then Ricky can at least see some pictures of it— (JANIE *exits Right.)*

CHARLES. I think I will take some pictures! *(Starts for hall)* There should still be film in the camera. *(Stops in hall.)*

ANNABELLE. *(Turning to him)* What is it?

CHARLES. *(Going to cupboard)* I just remembered— The camera's in the cupboard here.

ANNABELLE. Oh, no, I don't think so—

CHARLES. *(Turning knob)* Yes, I put it in here, I remember. It's locked. Where's the key?

ANNABELLE. Isn't it there?

CHARLES. *(Looking on floor for key)* No.

ANNABELLE. That's strange.

CHARLES. Yes, this hasn't been locked for years. Not since my father kept his Bourbon in it. The Bourbon that was too good for children. *(Goes to desk, looks in drawer.)*

(MILDRED *enters from hall.*)

ANNABELLE. I don't believe your camera's in there. You do mean the big one—the new one? *(Sees* MILDRED*)* Yes, Mildred?

CHARLES. *(Turning to* MILDRED*)* Oh, Mildred, have you seen the key to this cupboard?

MILDRED. No, sir. Isn't it there? It was the other day.

CHARLES. No, it's gone. *(Exits to hall.)*

ANNABELLE. It'll turn up. Yes, Mildred, what was it? Are you leaving now?

MILDRED. Cook and I both, yes.

ANNABELLE. Do you have a ride into town?

MILDRED. Fred's here. He's waiting.

ANNABELLE. Then you run along. Is Fred taking you to the carnival?

(CONNIE *enters Right.*)

MILDRED. Yes, he is. Well, good-bye, Miss Annabelle, and thank you for the afternoon off.

ANNABELLE. Why, don't you mention it. Just enjoy yourself.

(MILDRED *starts out.*)

CONNIE. Yes, Mildred, have fun.

MILDRED. Thank you, Mrs. Ashton. Good-bye. *(She exits to hall.)*

CONNIE. Well, I've got Janie under control. Now where's Charles?

ANNABELLE. About someplace.

CONNIE. He's not playing in the mud, I hope. *(Sits on sofa.)*

ANNABELLE. No, looking for his camera, I think. There are a few Auction calls I must make.

(She goes to desk, opens phone file as CHARLES *enters from hall with screwdriver and goes directly to cupboard.)*

CONNIE. Charles?

*(*ANNABELLE *picks up phone, starts to dial.)*

CHARLES. Huh?

CONNIE. What are you doing, darling?

CHARLES. We can't find the key to the cupboard.

ANNABELLE. *(Seeing* CHARLES *working on cupboard, hangs up)* What on earth! *(She steps to* CHARLES*)* Really, now!

CHARLES. It shouldn't be too hard to get this open.

ANNABELLE. But you're wasting your time! The camera isn't in there! I'm positive!

CHARLES. *(Working on lock)* Would you like to bet on that? *(Suddenly he pulls off doorknob. Returns front, holding it up)* Hey, have you ever seen half a doorknob?

CONNIE. Darling, you're tearing down our house.

CHARLES. I've always meant to tear it down. First minute I've had.

ANNABELLE. All this trouble. Tomorrow I'll get a locksmith—

CHARLES. It's no trouble. I enjoy this type of work. Breaking and entering.

ANNABELLE. But I tell you the camera isn't there! Connie, you remember—the Sunday before last—you and Charles went for a walk—

CONNIE. Yes—

ANNABELLE. You took the camera with you— Charles, do stop and listen to me!

CHARLES. I can hear you.

ANNABELLE. You remember taking the camera with you. Of course you do!

CHARLES. No, I didn't take it with me. *(He goes to desk, gets paperclip from drawer.)*

ANNABELLE. *(Moves to* CONNIE*)* Connie, you remember!

CONNIE. Yes, it seems to me he did take it.

ANNABELLE. And he didn't bring it back!

CONNIE. *(Rises)* Well, I hadn't thought about it— No, I don't think he did.

ANNABELLE. You stopped off somewhere—to see someone—

CONNIE. Yes, we did.

ANNABELLE. Charles might have left the camera there. Where did you stop? The Fergusons?

(CHARLES *goes to cupboard with paperclip.*)

CONNIE. No, I don't believe that was the name—but then I've met so many people lately.

ANNABELLE. *(Going to* CHARLES *at cupboard)* Charles! Was it the Fergusons?

CHARLES. *(Still at work, laughs)* Ferguson—Ferguson —that name's familiar.

ANNABELLE. Oh, no, Charles! Please answer me. Was it the Leonards? *(To* CONNIE*)* Connie, the Leonards?

CONNIE. That could have been it—tall people, both of them—three kids—

ANNABELLE. Yes! The Leonards! *(She goes to desk, sits, flips open file)* I'm just going to teach you a lesson. I'm going to prove to you how very wrong you can be at times. *(She is dialing)* I hope the Leonards are home—

CHARLES. It doesn't matter. I'll have this opened in a minute—

ANNABELLE. *(Into phone)* Hello, Claire—this is Annabelle Logan. I'm fine—how are you?

CHARLES. She isn't talking to Claire. *(To* CONNIE*)* She isn't talking to anyone.

ANNABELLE. *(Into phone)* Did Charles leave a camera at your place a few Sundays ago? Oh, would you? *(She looks to* CHARLES*)* You might as well stop. She's asking Sam.

CHARLES. *(To* CONNIE*)* That proves she's bluffing. Claire hasn't spoken to Sam for twenty years.

ANNABELLE. *(Rises. Into phone)* Yes, Claire?

CHARLES. Give me that phone. *(He takes it)* Hello—

(He is surprised) Claire? Is that you?—Well, is my camera there? All right, I'll stop over and get it. See you soon. *(He hangs up.)*

ANNABELLE. Well?

CHARLES. Okay, you can gloat.

ANNABELLE. Yes, I can and I should, but I simply haven't time. *(Going toward hall, turns back at door)* You ought to be getting off soon, too, Charles, especially if you're going to stop for your camera—which—is—at—the Leonards'—isn't it? *(She exits.)*

CHARLES. I was positive it was in there. *(Indicates cupboard)* I'll have to get a locksmith. *(To cupboard.)*

CONNIE. *(Rising)* Darling—

CHARLES. Yes?

CONNIE. *(Goes to* CHARLES) Take Ricky to the Carnival with you!

CHARLES. *(Puts screwdriver on desk)* Has Janie been needling you about that?

CONNIE. No, I'm asking for my sake. Take him, I want you to take him!

CHARLES. How the hell can I—after what he's done! *(*CHARLES *gets envelope from drawer, puts knob in it.)*

CONNIE. Darling, the way things are between Ricky and me, he shouldn't be punished now, not today!

CHARLES. *(Putting envelope into drawer and closing it)* We can't overlook this! Connie!

CONNIE. Up till now Ricky's merely resented me—I hope. But now at this moment he's up in his room hating me! He's being punished because of me. He blames me for not being able to work on his boat, for having to stay in his room—for missing the carnival—oh, darling, this isn't the way to handle it, it's much too drastic.

CHARLES. What he did was a little drastic. *(Picks up screwdriver and puts it in drawer.)*

CONNIE. Darling, I'm frightened about Ricky and me! I was hoping I could handle it alone— I was sure I could, but I'm not sure now. Somehow it's got away from me, and I need your help! Please—

(RICKY *enters Right.)*

Oh, hello, Ricky. *(She turns quickly back to* Charles.*)*
    Charles. Hiya, Rick.
    Ricky. Miss Annabelle said I could work on my boat.
I don't have to stay in my room any more.

(Connie *and* Charles *exchange looks.)*

    Charles. Rick—
    Ricky. What?
    Charles. *(Goes to* Ricky*)* Look—in California—we
had a good time out there—you and Janie and Connie and
I—we had a lot of fun together, didn't we?
    (Ricky *nods his head.)*
But here—something's gone wrong here. We're going to
fix that and start all over as if nothing ever went wrong.
But first—about what happened today—we've got to fix
that first. That was a bad mistake you made—but lots of
people make mistakes—why people make so many mistakes they should have rubber heads like pencils— You
know, erasers, so they can correct their own mistakes.
    Ricky. *(Not smiling)* Yes, sir.
    Charles. So you make a mistake today. That was too
bad. But it's even worse not to tell the truth, not to admit
your mistake and apologize. You're being kept at home
today—not just because of what you did to Connie's
dress, but because you didn't tell the truth. Now if you'll
admit it and tell Connie you're sorry—you can go to the
carnival.

(A pause before Ricky *speaks.* Annabelle *appears in
    hall doorway. She is wearing a sweater. She listens,
    unseen.)*

    Ricky. You mean—all I have to do is say I ripped her
dress and tell her I'm sorry?
    Charles. Yes. And I'll take you with us this after-
noon—and somehow I'll make sure that tomorrow you
see the Death Defying Leap into the Pool of Fire!
    Ricky. *(Agonized)* Gee—
    Connie. Ricky, you needn't apologize to me—we want
you to go to the carnival.

RICKY. *(Turns front and very lowly)* Okay— I cut up your dress—

CHARLES. What did you say, Rick?

RICKY. I cut up her dress.

CONNIE. *(Goes to* RICKY) Ricky, it's all right now— it's all over. Nothing ever happened. You go to the carnival and have a wonderful time. That was a brave thing you just did. You've earned yourself a wonderful time. *(She rumples his hair.)*

RICKY. *(Pulls back from her)* Don't touch me!

(CONNIE *is stunned.*)

CHARLES. *(His shock explodes in anger)* Ricky!

RICKY. I don't care! I didn't tear her old dress! I never even saw her old dress! *(He starts running toward terrace)* I don't want to go to the damn carnival! *(He runs out.)*

CHARLES. *(Starts to follow him)* Ricky, come back here—

CONNIE. No, Charles—not now—

(ANNABELLE *steps back out of sight in hall doorway as* CHARLES *turns to* CONNIE. *There is a slight pause.)*

ANNABELLE. *(Offstage)* Janie! Janie, dear, hurry! Daddy's waiting for you. (ANNABELLE *enters)* Well, I'm off to Mrs. Walworth's. Oh, Charles, I've told Ricky he might play with his boat.

CHARLES. *(Turning to* ANNABELLE) Yes, I know. *(He goes to terrace door, looks for* RICKY.)

ANNABELLE. I thought it was going a bit too far to keep the child indoors on such a beautiful day. Connie, it's much too nice to have to go to New York—but then, I suppose you will have fun. I'll be watching your show tonight, darling.

CONNIE. Thank you, Annabelle.

ANNABELLE. 'Bye, bye, dears.

(ANNABELLE *exits to hall as* JANIE *enters Right.)*

CONNIE. Oh, there you are, Janie, why you look pretty enough to go to a carnival.

JANIE. I am going to a carnival.

CONNIE. I know you are.

JANIE. Let's go, Daddy.

CHARLES. Yes, darling. You wait in the car for me. I'll be right out.

JANIE. Okay. *(Starts for terrace.)*

CONNIE. Have a good time, sweetie.

JANIE. Thank you, 'bye! *(She exits.)*

CHARLES. *(Goes to* CONNIE*)* Connie—

CONNIE. Darling, thank you for trying—

CHARLES. *(Takes her in his arms)* Look, you go to New York and have yourself a little vacation from the Ashton family. You deserve it.

CONNIE. No, I wish I hadn't promised to do this silly television thing. I'll hurry back.

(They kiss.)

JANIE. *(Off Left)* Come on, Daddy!

(CHARLES *releases* CONNIE *and exits quickly to terrace. CONNIE follows him to door, stands watching for a moment, then moves to desk. She pauses uncertainly for a moment, then looks at clock and exits to hall. The CLOCK strikes three. The stage is empty for several moments.* CONNIE *re-enters from hall with her purse. She sits on sofa, takes cigarette case from her purse, begins to fill it from box on coffee table. The PHONE rings.* CONNIE *goes to desk.)*

CONNIE. *(Into phone)* Hello— No, this is Mrs. Ashton. Oh, yes, Mrs. Weaver, we met the other day—the picture. Why, thank you— I hope the auction is a big success. Annabelle just left a few minutes ago. She went over to Mrs. Walworth's— She'll be back about four-thirty— wouldn't you like her to call you? Oh, all right, good-bye, Mrs. Weaver. *(She hangs up, then goes back to the coffee table. She finishes filling her cigarette case. She is putting it in her purse when she hears a noise)* Ricky? *(She starts for hall and sees* RICKY *out on the terrace)* Oh—hi.

RICKY. *(Steps into doorway)* Are you busy?

CONNIE. No—you wanted to talk to me?

RICKY. Yes— *(Now he's a little timid)* But if you're busy, I can come back later.

CONNIE. No, stick around, talk to me. *(Her attitude is consciously casual)* Everybody's gone but us.

RICKY. *(Goes to* CONNIE, *pulling a bank book in case from his back pocket. He thrusts it into* CONNIE'S *hands)* Here, take it.

CONNIE. *(Takes it, sits on arm of chair. Reads)* "The First National Bank and Trust Company." *(Takes out book)* "In account with Richard Wells Ashton—"

RICKY. *(Matter of fact)* Wells—that was my mother's name before it was Ashton. Elizabeth Wells.

CONNIE. Yes, I know. *(Looks at book)* "One hundred and eighteen dollars and seventy-two cents."

RICKY. It's mine. I can do whatever I want with it.

CONNIE. I'm sure you can. Did you earn it?

RICKY. Part of it. I want you to use it. To buy a ticket to California.

CONNIE. Oh!

RICKY. It's enough, isn't it?

CONNIE. Yes—

RICKY. How soon can you get ready?

CONNIE. Pretty quickly. I guess you'd help me pack, wouldn't you?

RICKY. I couldn't help you much. I'm not allowed in your room. I'm never to go in it again.

CONNIE. Who said so?

RICKY. Miss Annabelle. I'm allowed to go any place I want in the whole house except your room. Are you going back to California? To Hollywood?

CONNIE. *(Rises)* I guess I'd better, Rick.

RICKY. You could sleep in California.

CONNIE. *(Puzzled; smiles)* I'm sleeping all right here.

RICKY. I mean in the mornings. You could sleep till noon. You wouldn't be able to hear me in California.

CONNIE. Hear you?

RICKY. Make so much noise. I know actresses aren't like other people.

CONNIE. Miss Annabelle tell you that?

RICKY. *(Nods)* It isn't your fault. You aren't used to children.

CONNIE. *(A laugh)* Ricky. *(Sits on sofa)* When I was working in a picture, which in the past twelve years has been almost always, I got up at five o'clock in the morning.

RICKY. Then you must be tired. And I keep you awake.

CONNIE. *(Laughs)* I'm not tired. Do I look tired?

RICKY. No. *(A simple statement, not flattery)* You look pretty good. I always liked you in the movies.

CONNIE. It's just around the house, huh?

RICKY. Aren't you kind of anxious to get back? *(Indicates bankbook)* You can use that till you get a job again. You will be able to get a job, won't you?

CONNIE. I guess so. But— Don't worry about it. And I'll pay you back out of my first week's salary.

RICKY. It isn't a loan. I'm giving it to you.

CONNIE. Well, thanks again.

RICKY. *(Gravely)* Don't mention it. It's a pleasure. When will you be going?

CONNIE. Well, let's see— I've got this television thing tonight—

RICKY. Daddy said Janie and I could stay up to see you.

CONNIE. Oh, I don't know if it'll be worth it. You won't get to bed till ten o'clock. Of course, if you want to sleep in the morning, I'll be real quiet.

RICKY. *(Smiles)* Nobody can wake me up.

CONNIE. I know! Nine-year-old boys aren't like other people.

RICKY. *(Moves to sofa slowly)* I want to see you to-night. I saw you once before on television. A movie. You shot Richard Widmark.

CONNIE. Sorry about that. But he had it coming to him.

RICKY. Sure! He was asking for it!

CONNIE. Askin' for it? He was beggin' for it! The double-crossin' rat!

RICKY. *(Sits beside her on sofa)* How many times did you shoot him?

CONNIE. As I recall, I emptied my gun into him.

RICKY. That would be six times. You only had one gun, didn't you?

CONNIE. Yes. Cheap picture. You do like movies, don't you?

RICKY. Some of them. I like sailing more than anything.

CONNIE. I like sailing. Fun.

RICKY. Do you like baseball? I do. Do you?

CONNIE. No.

RICKY. Oh, I think it's pretty good.

CONNIE. I don't like base, basket or volley ball.

RICKY. Do you like foot?

CONNIE. High school, college or professional foot?

RICKY. Well, high school, for instance.

CONNIE. Oh—it's okay.

RICKY. College?

CONNIE. Oh—it's okay.

RICKY. Professional?

CONNIE. Professional American or professional Canadian?

RICKY. Well, professional American.

CONNIE. Which league?

RICKY. There's only one.

CONNIE. There is not! There are two leagues! Just like big league baseball.

RICKY. No. One league with two divisions.

CONNIE. How much do you want to bet?

RICKY. *(Picks up bankbook from sofa)* A hundred and eighteen dollars and seventy-two cents.

CONNIE. Say, listen, how would you like to go to New York with me?

RICKY. When?

CONNIE. Now! Right away! We've got a lot to talk about. You know, this is the first time we've ever been alone together for more than a minute.

RICKY. You mean I could go to the television studio with you?

CONNIE. Sure. You want to?

RICKY. *(Rising)* Yes! *(Then shakes his head)* No, I'd be in your way.

CONNIE. If you're in the way, I'll tell you to move over. *(She rises)* Let's take an earlier train. How long will it take you to get ready? A half-hour? Can we make the three forty-five?

RICKY. Easy, sure, but—

CONNIE. What?

RICKY. I'm not supposed to go anywhere! Listen, I didn't tear your dress!

CONNIE. Ricky— Let's not even think about that any more. *(She puts arm around him, moves away from sofa with him)* We'll leave a note for your father. We can see a movie—maybe even Radio City—and we'll still have lots of time for dinner. Any restaurant in town, you name it! Where would you like to eat?

RICKY. Chock Full O' Nuts.

CONNIE. All right. Let's get moving.

RICKY. I have to fix my paint cans.

CONNIE. Well, hurry up. *(Starts him toward terrace)* I'll call a cab.

(As RICKY *dashes out,* CONNIE *goes to the phone. She is starting to dial when she hears* RICKY.*)*

RICKY. *(Off Left)* Hey, Connie!
    *(*CONNIE *hangs up phone and hides behind chair.)*
*(*RICKY *enters)* Hey, Connie!

CONNIE. *(Rising from behind chair)* Lissen, pardner—

RICKY. *(Wheeling to her, laughing)* Hey!

CONNIE. Never turn your back on an overstuffed chair.

RICKY. Okay!

CONNIE. What are you doing here? What about your paint cans?

RICKY. Do I have to take a bath?

CONNIE. I'd say so. It might take you all of two minutes. What did you have in mind?

RICKY. Well—I need one, but on second thought—you going to take one?

CONNIE. I've had mine. I felt as though I should. You know, television. I'm going to be invited into millions of living rooms.

RICKY. Okay, what the hell, I'll take one, too! And should I wear my good clothes?

CONNIE. Well, I am. In fact, since this is our first date, I'm going to wear my very best clothes.

RICKY. Okay. So will I!

CONNIE. Okay!

(They shake hands.)

Well, get going!

(He runs out Right. CONNIE goes to phone, dials. The line is busy. She hangs up, takes piece of paper and starts to write note. ANNABELLE enters from hall. She has CONNIE's fur coat over her arm.)

ANNABELLE. Connie, dear—

CONNIE. *(Turning quickly)* Annabelle!—You scared me! You're not back from Mrs. Walworth's already?

ANNABELLE. Such a silly thing. So clumsy of me. I twisted my ankle.

CONNIE. Oh, I'm sorry. Shouldn't you lie down or—

ANNABELLE. No, no, it's not as bad as all that. It's such a long walk, though, I was afraid to risk it. So, I turned back. I thought we'd put your furs away now. We've procrastinated long enough. *(She puts fur coat on back of chair.)*

CONNIE. Thanks, Annabelle, that's nice of you. *(She is writing again)* I'm leaving a note for Charles. I'm taking Ricky into New York with me.

ANNABELLE. *(On her way to vault, stops)* Taking him with you! Why, how can you? He's being punished! You know that. *(She closes hall door, goes to vault.)*

CONNIE. I'm in a rush now, I'll explain later. I know you'll understand—

ANNABELLE. *(Opens louvered doors, dials combination, and opens steel doors. She turns to CONNIE)* Connie, dear, do put your furs away. Such lovely furs—you shouldn't be careless of them.

CONNIE. *(Finishing note)* I really must hurry, Annabelle. We want to catch the train and I have to finish dressing. I wonder would you mind doing it for me?

ANNABELLE. Why, of course not. *(She gets fur coat from chair.)*

CONNIE. It's dreadful of me to impose on you this way, I know— *(She is going to hall doors.)*

(ANNABELLE *with coat is just a step behind* CONNIE. *As* CONNIE *reaches hall door,* ANNABELLE *pretends to trip and falls.)*

ANNABELLE. *(As she falls utters a sharp cry)* Connie—
CONNIE. *(Turns quickly to* ANNABELLE*)* Annabelle—
ANNABELLE. My ankle— I can't move—
CONNIE. I'm sorry—
ANNABELLE. Take this, put it in the vault!
CONNIE. Let me help you up.
ANNABELLE. *(Vehemently)* Put it in the vault—don't worry about me. I'll be all right in a minute. Don't fuss!
CONNIE. *(Takes coat)* Of course. I'm sorry.

(CONNIE *steps into vault with coat.* ANNABELLE *springs to her feet and slams shut the steel door, cutting off* CONNIE'S *scream.* ANNABELLE *quickly closes louvered doors. She leans against doors for a moment, then she hears* RICKY.*)*

RICKY. *(Offstage Right)* Hey, Connie.
(ANNABELLE *hesitates a moment, then steps out the hall doors and out of sight as* RICKY *enters through the door.)*
Connie! *(He stands for a moment, looking around)* I know you're hiding. *(He looks behind armchair, then looks behind desk. Then he runs out through hall in the opposite direction* ANNABELLE *took)* Hey, Connie, we'll miss our train. *(He is out.)*

(A pause and ANNABELLE *enters through hall door. She*

goes directly to desk and gets CONNIE'S *note, crumples it and starts out terrace doors; remembers, and gets* CONNIE'S *purse from coffee table. She exits through terrace doors.)*

RICKY. *(In hall)* Connie! *(A pause, then he enters)* Hey, Connie, where are you? *(He pauses for a moment looking around the room. He slowly sinks disgustedly into chair)* Damn women!

CURTAIN

ACT THREE

The library.

The same afternoon. Five o'clock.

*At rise the room is empty, the hall door is closed. The
purple glads are in a vase on coffee table. Two of
them are on coffee table, ready to be placed in vase.
There is some fern near the vase.* ANNABELLE *enters
from the hall wearing a housecoat. The* CLOCK
*strikes five. She stops, standing still until the clock
strike finishes, then she turns slowly to the vault.
She looks at it for a moment, then she gets scissors
from sheath on desk and goes to coffee table. She picks
up a piece of fern, and snips it for arranging it with
the glads. She places it in the metal vase, then picks
up another fern. She trims it and as she places it in
the vase, the front DOOR is heard to slam. She sits
on sofa, continuing to arrange the flowers as* JANIE
enters through the hall door.

JANIE. Hello, we're home. *(She enters carrying a pin-
wheel and a gas-filled balloon on a light string.)*
ANNABELLE. Hello there. Where's your father?
JANIE. Putting the car away.
ANNABELLE. You're back so soon!
JANIE. I got sick at my stomach. I ate too much pop-
corn.
ANNABELLE. Oh, Janie! Perhaps you should lie down
for a little.
JANIE. I'm all right now.

ANNABELLE. Well, be quiet a while. Tell me, what did you like best about the carnival?

JANIE. The popcorn.

ANNABELLE. *(Laughs)* You are loyal, aren't you? Did your father take lots and lots of pictures?

JANIE. He let me take some, too. We took pictures of everything!

ANNABELLE. Then you did have some fun.

JANIE. Oh, yes!

ANNABELLE. Thank you, Miss Annabelle.

JANIE. Oh, yes! Thank you, Miss Annabelle.

(JANIE *sits as* CHARLES *enters from terrace. He is carrying white yachting cap and pirate's flag.)*

ANNABELLE. Hello Charles! You didn't have too much popcorn, did you?

CHARLES. *(Laughing)* No, I didn't, but—that little one there—

ANNABELLE. Yes.

CHARLES. Where's Ricky? I've been looking for him. He isn't down at the pond.

ANNABELLE. He's up in his room. He'll be down in a minute, I'm sure.

CHARLES. How is he?

ANNABELLE. He's being a brave little boy. Would you like a drink?

CHARLES. *(Puts present on desk)* I don't think so. Did those blueprints come back from the printers yet?

ANNABELLE. Just a bit ago. They're on the hall table.

CHARLES. *(Gets the sketches from the hall table)* Good. I want to take them to Pawling tomorrow. Connie get off all right?

ANNABELLE. I imagine. She'd left by the time I got back from Mrs. Walworth's.

CHARLES. You have a good time?

ANNABELLE. Yes. She's such an amusing person, Mrs. Walworth is.

CHARLES. *(Sitting at desk)* You're going to miss her when you're in London.

ANNABELLE. I shall. You know I shall.

CHARLES. *(Picking up letter from desk)* What's this? Doctor Lindstrum—the report on Connie's dog. *(Reads slowly)* The dog was suffocated— *(To* ANNABELLE*)* Suffocated? How could that have happened?

(JANIE *rises and goes to vault.)*

ANNABELLE. I don't understand it.
(At vault, JANIE *ties her balloon to a handle of the louvered door.)*
(ANNABELLE *puts finishing touches on glads, rises)* There. Aren't they lovely?
(JANIE *starts slowly toward door Right.)*
(ANNABELLE *picks up vase of flowers and puts them on the sofa's end table. Suddenly she sees the balloon)* Janie!

JANIE. *(At doorway Right)* I'm going to give Ricky my pinwheel.

ANNABELLE. *(Her composure somewhat regained)* That's my good, generous girl.

JANIE. It makes me dizzy. *(She exits.)*

CHARLES. Good, generous girl. Carnivals, it seems, don't build character. Well, I guess I'd better go up and talk to him.

ANNABELLE. *(Crossing to* CHARLES. *Earnestly)* Oh, Charles, you're not still worried about Ricky and Connie, are you? Please try not to.

CHARLES. *(Grimly looking at yachting cap)* I'll try to worry just the right amount.

ANNABELLE. *(Sighs)* Sometimes little boys can be so cruel. Or is that too strong a word?

CHARLES. Annabelle, *you* try not to worry too much.

ANNABELLE. *(Putting hand on his shoulder)* Oh, dear, we are upset, all of us, aren't we?

CHARLES. Yes. We are upset. That was an upsetting thing Ricky did. I wouldn't call that too strong a word.

ANNABELLE. I know. And just when things seemed to be going so well. I was certain Connie had just about won him over. That's what distresses me most—that I could have been so very wrong—

(She breaks off as RICKY *enters from Right.)*

RICKY. *(Sullen, hostile)* Janie said you wanted to see me.

CHARLES. *(Rising. Picking up presents)* As a matter of fact I was just coming up to see you.

RICKY. What for?

CHARLES. I just wanted to say hello. Come in.
(RICKY *comes in.)*
Work on your boat this afternoon?

RICKY. Some.

CHARLES. How's it coming?

RICKY. Okay.

CHARLES. About ready to be launched, I bet.

RICKY. I guess so.

CHARLES. You guess so? You're the Captain.

RICKY. You don't care! What are you asking me for?

(ANNABELLE *and* CHARLES *exchange glances.)*

CHARLES. Ricky, I do care—

RICKY. *(Going to* ANNABELLE) Miss Annabelle!

ANNABELLE. What is it, dear?

RICKY. Take me to London with you!

ANNABELLE. Darling, you don't mean that!

RICKY. I do! I want to get out of here!

ANNABELLE. Now, Ricky—

RICKY. Nobody believes a word I say around here! You all think I'm a liar! But I'm not. I— Other people lie, though! They lie to me and nothing happens to them! They don't get punished!

CHARLES. Ricky, who lied to you?

RICKY. Connie!

CHARLES. *(Puts yachting cap and flag on desk and goes to* RICKY) You must have misunderstood her, Ricky. She wouldn't lie to you. Tell me about it— I bet we can straighten it out.

RICKY. No! I hate her! I wish she was dead!

ANNABELLE. Ricky!

(The DOORBELL rings.)

CHARLES. *(Grasping* RICKY *by both arms)* Son, listen to me! *(Sits on chair still holding* RICKY*)* We all get mad at each other sometimes. And that temper of yours—it's awful big for such a little guy, but I know where you got it— *(Jerks a thumb at himself)* But half the time when I get mad at someone—it's for nothing—I made a mistake —I was wrong—

RICKY. *(Backing away) Connie* made the mistake! *She* lied.

> *(Pulling away from* CHARLES, *he crosses to* ANNA-
> BELLE, *hugs her.* CHARLES *rises, faces them.)*

Please, please take me to London with you, please—

CHARLES. Now, Ricky, tell me what happened—

> *(The DOORBELL rings again.)*

Damn it— *(He exits into hall.)*

ANNABELLE. *(Sitting)* Now, you come and tell Miss Annabelle what really happened.

RICKY. She did lie! She promised to take me to New York with her and then she went without me.

ANNABELLE. Oh, no—no, dear. You were being punished—and your punishment was staying at home. Connie knew that. She never would have promised to take you—

RICKY. But she did! Honest! *(Desperately)* Don't *you* believe me, Miss Annabelle?

ANNABELLE. Of course I do. But I'm terribly afraid that other people might think that— *(She stops, lets* RICKY *get it.)*

RICKY. You mean Daddy. He won't believe me.

ANNABELLE. Well, now—

RICKY. You're right. He'll just think I'm lying again.

ANNABELLE. I'm afraid so. And another little lie might mean more punishment. So I wouldn't say anything about Connie promising to take you with her. Ricky—

RICKY. Yes?

ANNABELLE. *(Conspiratorially)* Suppose we keep this a secret, you and I.

RICKY. Okay! I'm not going to get punished for nothing again!

ANNABELLE. *(Quickly, hearing* CHARLES *returning)* We won't tell a soul, will we?

RICKY. No!

*(*CHARLES *enters from hall, followed by a young man of about thirty.)*

CHARLES. Ricky, would you go to your room for a few minutes, please?

RICKY. Yes sir. *(He exits Right.)*

*(*ANNABELLE *rises.)*

CHARLES. This is Detective Lieutenant Mitchell, Annabelle. Lieutenant, Miss Logan.

MITCHELL. Miss Logan.

ANNABELLE. Detective Lieutenant—the police? What's gone wrong?

CHARLES. Bad news, I'm afraid. *(Goes to* ANNABELLE, *gently)* It's Mrs. Walworth. She was hit by a car. She's dead, Annabelle.

*(*ANNABELLE *sinks into a chair.)*
*(*CHARLES *mistakes her realization that her alibi is gone for grief)* I'm sorry. I know what a shock this is.

ANNABELLE. Yes— Charles, if I could have some water, please—

CHARLES. Yes— *(Exits quickly to hall.)*

MITCHELL. I'm sorry that I—

ANNABELLE. No, no— *(Urgently)* Tell me—when did it happen?

MITCHELL. Just this afternoon.

ANNABELLE. *(Tensely)* What time this afternoon?

MITCHELL. About one-thirty.

*(*ANNABELLE *stiffens, then covers up by turning away, pretending to be grief-stricken.)*
I'm sorry I had to come barging in like this—

ANNABELLE. No, I shouldn't have let myself go like this. But it is such a shock—

MITCHELL. Of course.

ANNABELLE. Mrs. Walworth and I. We were so very close—the poor soul, where was she?

MITCHELL. King's Highway—near the airport—
    (CHARLES *enters with glass of water.*)
—it seems she'd been drinking—
CHARLES. *(Giving her water)* Here you are.
ANNABELLE. Thank you. *(She sips the water)* I'll be all right now, Charles.
CHARLES. Are you sure?
ANNABELLE. Yes, quite all right—
CHARLES. *(To MITCHELL)* How did it happen? You said Mrs. Walworth had been drinking?

(ANNABELLE *is tense, watchful, dreading the mention of the time of* MRS. WALWORTH'S *death in* CHARLES' *presence.*)

MITCHELL. Quite a lot. She went into a bar on King's Highway, the bartender refused to serve her. She raised quite a fuss, she was pretty drunk, I'm afraid. When she left she started across the street to another bar. She stepped right in front of a car. The driver didn't have a chance to avoid her—the bartender saw it happen.
ANNABELLE. How horrible—
CHARLES. *(Puzzled)* I knew she drank some, but I didn't realize it was that bad. Did you notice, Annabelle?
ANNABELLE. *(Quickly)* No. But then, up to a certain point, she was always in perfect control. The poor thing —did she suffer?
MITCHELL. No, she died instantly. Miss Logan, we're hoping you can help us. *(Takes notebook out from inside jacket pocket)* A neighbor of hers told us you've known Mrs. Walworth a long time.
ANNABELLE. *(Nods)* Almost all my life.
MITCHELL. You're not related to her?
ANNABELLE. No.
MITCHELL. We're trying to locate her family—some relative to notify of her death.
ANNABELLE. I'm not sure I can help you—
MITCHELL. *(Referring to notebook)* Her husband, Harry Walworth. Do you know anything about him?
ANNABELLE. I never knew him. They've been separ-

ated for a long time. I have the impression that she lost all track of him years ago.

MITCHELL. What about relatives?

ANNABELLE. None in this country, I'm sure of that. She was English, you know.

MITCHELL. Yes. Her family's there, then.

ANNABELLE. If there is a family—it seems she spoke once or twice of a sister—no, I can't even be sure of that. It's sad, isn't it, that anyone could be so alone?

MITCHELL. She still heard from somebody in England. *(He takes letter from his pocket)* This letter was in her purse. The return address is— *(He reads it)* 17 Melville Street, Knightsbridge, London, S.W. 1— The writing is obviously a woman's and I think the signature is Lucinda. Does that name mean anything to you, Miss Logan?

(ANNABELLE *rises slowly.* CHARLES *moves to* MITCHELL.)

CHARLES. Lucinda—that name's familiar—yes, Elizabeth used to speak of a Lucinda— Lucinda Marsh, wasn't it?

ANNABELLE. Of course, Lucinda Marsh. Yes!

MITCHELL. She isn't related to Mrs. Walworth?

ANNABELLE. No, no, Mrs. Walworth was Lucinda's nurse way back in England—when Lucinda was a child.

MITCHELL. *(To* CHARLES) You mentioned Elizabeth, Mr. Ashton. That name's here in the letter.

CHARLES. My wife. She died several years ago.

MITCHELL. I see. And then she mentions a Beebee here—

(CHARLES *starts to answer when he is interrupted by* ANNABELLE.)

ANNABELLE. Lieutenant—we were such dear friends in the old days, Lucinda and I, we both adored Mrs. Walworth so. It would be much less painful for Lucinda to hear about the accident from me—rather than the police.

MITCHELL. I'm sure it would.

ANNABELLE. May I have that letter— *(She extends her hand to him)* I'll just copy down the address—

(He gives her the letter.)
Thank you. Such a sad letter for me to write— *(She is crossing to desk)* It will be a shock to Lucinda. Just think—she was still writing to Mrs. Walworth after all these years. Such devotion. If only I could have done more. *(She sits at desk.)*

CHARLES. *(To* MITCHELL*)* Hardly a week passed without Miss Logan visiting Mrs. Walworth. *(Crossing to behind* ANNABELLE*)* I'm glad things worked out so that you could be with her this afternoon. *(He places hand gently on her shoulder.)*

MITCHELL. This afternoon—you saw Mrs. Walworth this afternoon?

ANNABELLE. *(Rising)* Why, yes, I did.

MITCHELL. What time was that?

ANNABELLE. Well, let me see— It was—usually I go for tea, but today things were so confusing here—I don't know exactly—

CHARLES. You left here when Janie and I did. You must have got to her house a little after three.

MITCHELL. But Mrs. Walworth died about half-past one. I told Miss Logan that.

*(*ANNABELLE *sits.)*
In fact, the call came into Headquarters at one-thirty-five.

CHARLES. That isn't possible. I'm positive Miss Logan didn't leave here until after that. You must be wrong.

MITCHELL. No sir. It's in the records at Headquarters —one-thirty-five. *(To* ANNABELLE*)* Miss Logan—

CHARLES. *(Going to* MITCHELL*)* Just a minute. Who identified Mrs. Walworth?

MITCHELL. Why?

CHARLES. You say she died at one-thirty, but Miss Logan saw her later than that. She spent the afternoon with her. I don't know how it could have happened, but there must have been a mistake in identification. It must have been someone else in the accident.

MITCHELL. *(Taking notebook from breast pocket)* No, sir.

CHARLES. I know you found Mrs. Walworth's purse, but—

MITCHELL. *(Shakes his head)* There's been no mistake. A neighbor made positive identification. The woman was Ethel Walworth and she died at one-thirty this afternoon.

CHARLES. Annabelle—

ANNABELLE. *(She rises, turns slowly)* Charles, Mr. Mitchell, I seem to have made matters worse, not better as I had hoped. Oh, dear—I'm sorry. I'll have to explain. *(She shakes her head)* I didn't go to Mrs. Walworth's at all.

CHARLES. But you said you did.

ANNABELLE. Oh, I meant to go— I started out for her house— *(To MITCHELL)* When I started thinking about Mrs. Ashton alone here with Ricky. Ricky, that's—

MITCHELL. The boy?

ANNABELLE. Yes. *(To CHARLES)* Charles, I was much more upset over what happened this morning than I let you know. To think that Ricky had become capable of so vicious an act— I was deeply concerned. So concerned that I didn't go to Ethel Walworth's. I turned around and came back to see if Connie—if Connie and Ricky were getting along all right—

CHARLES. What did you think could happen?

ANNABELLE. *(Going to MITCHELL)* You see, Lieutenant, Ricky blamed Connie for missing the carnival today. —That was how we punished him for deliberately ruining —slashing with a knife Mrs. Ashton's dress. It seemed to make him more resentful than ever—as though it were Connie who had punished him, not us. I thought perhaps it was a mistake to leave them alone together all afternoon—

CHARLES. It was a mistake.

ANNABELLE. *(Turning to CHARLES)* No, Charles! Listen to me, let me finish. I was wrong, happily, I was wrong. When I got back here there was Ricky down at the pond playing nice as you please. I was ashamed. I took myself for a long walk and gave myself a good talking to for jumping to such—such ridiculous conclusions.

CHARLES. They weren't entirely ridiculous! You heard the way Ricky was carrying on. *(He turns away from* ANNABELLE.*)*

ANNABELLE. Charles, he's a little boy! When he says he hates Connie and wishes she were dead—he's only a child, making wild, extravagant statements—that's all!

(CHARLES *turns to her, starts to speak, but she continues.)*

Oh, can't we discuss this later? Mr. Mitchell's being very patient about our little problem, but I imagine he—

MITCHELL. No, it's all right. *(Glances at wrist watch)* Almost five-thirty. I ought to be getting back to Headquarters. Sorry I had to bring you bad news—but thanks for your help.

CHARLES. Take a short cut to your car across the terrace.

MITCHELL. *(Starting for hall)* Thanks I will—but my hat, I left it in the hall.

CHARLES. I'll get it. *(He exits to hall.)*

ANNABELLE. I seem to have upset Mr. Ashton. The very thing I wished to avoid—lying about my being at Mrs. Walworth's— *(She is at table, touching up flowers)* How very stupid of me!

MITCHELL. *(Awkwardly)* No— wouldn't say that— *(Changing subject, nods towards flowers)* Nice, aren't they? Unusual color.

ANNABELLE. Yes, they are unusual. *(Moves away from flowers.)*

MITCHELL. Funny thing. I don't remember ever seeing flowers that color before. And this is the second time today. *(Thinking)* Now where was it—

ANNABELLE. *(Quickly)* Lieutenant, tell me—

MITCHELL. Oh, yes! At Mrs. Walworth's place, of course. A whole corner of the garden—

ANNABELLE. Yes—it was she who gave us the bulbs so that we might grow our own.

CHARLES. *(Enters from hall. To* MITCHELL) Here you

are. *(Handing hat to* MITCHELL*)* I'll walk to your car with you. *(He starts* MITCHELL *toward terrace.)*
MITCHELL. Good-bye, Miss Logan.
ANNABELLE. Good-bye, Lieutenant.

(MITCHELL *and* CHARLES *exit.* ANNABELLE *has a moment of near panic. She turns to the vault, then rushes to it. Viciously she rips the balloon from the louvered door. She takes it to the terrace, releases it. As she watches it rise above the trees, her composure returns. She remembers the letter on the desk. Quickly, she looks through and she is horrified to see how incriminating it is. She crumples it up and, as she hears* CHARLES *coming back, she thrusts it into her purse on the desk. When* CHARLES *enters she is at the coffee table, straightening it up.* CHARLES *goes directly to the phone, dials the Operator.)*

ANNABELLE. Charles, what is it?
CHARLES. *(Into phone)* Operator— New York— Atwater 9-1434— *(To* ANNABELLE*)* I want to find out what went on here this afternoon.
ANNABELLE. Whom are you phoning?
CHARLES. Connie. She ought to be at Betsy McLane's by now—
ANNABELLE. But is it necessary to worry her before her television show—she's nervous enough without you— Charles, talk to Ricky, why don't you?
CHARLES. I feel as though I've spent the day cross-examining that kid. *(Into phone)* This is Westford 9-6858. *(Back to* ANNABELLE*)* I want to explain to him why he's wrong—that Connie didn't lie to him. *(Into phone)* Hello— Betsy, hello. This is Charles Ashton— Fine, thanks.
(ANNABELLE *listens tensely.)*
Is Connie there? She isn't? She ought to have got to your place by now—yes, she was planning to stop in on her way to the broadcast tonight. Didn't she phone you? Well, she must have changed her mind, then. No—no, it's not important— Yes, I'll tell her. So long. *(He hangs up.)*

ANNABELLE. *(Relaxing)* I didn't think she planned to stop at Betsy's. I believe she was just going to have an early dinner, then go straight on to the studio.

CHARLES. She took the four-eighteen, didn't she?

ANNABELLE. I think that's what she said. Yes, the four-eighteen. Why?

CHARLES. That gets to New York at five-ten.

ANNABELLE. I think so.

CHARLES. That gives her three hours before she has to be at the studio.

ANNABELLE. She wanted to give herself plenty of time.

CHARLES. Three hours? *(He turns to go to desk as* MITCHELL *appears in terrace doorway)* Oh, Lieutenant.

MITCHELL. Sorry to bother you again. That letter from England—I left it here.

CHARLES. Oh, yes, Annabelle, the letter.

ANNABELLE. Of course. I should have returned it to you— *(She goes to desk, begins to search top of it)* I left it on the desk when I copied the address—

> (CHARLES *goes to chair below desk, sits and picks up* > *phone.)*

I'm terribly sorry, Lieutenant.

MITCHELL. It's all right. I only got as far as the high-way.

CHARLES. Excuse me— *(He is dialing phone.)*

ANNABELLE. Charles! What are you up to now?

CHARLES. Calling the taxi people.

ANNABELLE. Why?

CHARLES. Connie might have taken a later train— that's why she's not at Betsy's— *(Into phone)* Hello, this is Charles Ashton. My wife used one of your cabs to get to the station this afternoon. Could you tell me which train she caught? I'll hold on—

ANNABELLE. Charles, why are you so worried?

CHARLES. Let's not keep the Lieutenant waiting, Annabelle.

ANNABELLE. Oh, sorry. I just don't seem to be able to find it. Heavens, the condition I've let this desk get into!

(She is tidying the desk as she searches for the letter. She puts bills, correspondence into a letter box, her purse into a drawer. MITCHELL watches her; CHARLES is more involved with the phone call.)

CHARLES. *(Into phone)* That's all right— I'll wait—

ANNABELLE. Where can it be? Things don't simply vanish into thin air!

MITCHELL. *(Looking at her closely)* No, they don't.

ANNABELLE. Oh, here—here's the address! *(Holds it up)* That's all you wanted, isn't it? Lucinda's address. Isn't it lucky I wrote it down! Here you are! *(Extends it to him.)*

MITCHELL. *(Not taking it)* Don't you want to make a copy of it? You were so anxious to write to your friend.

ANNABELLE. Oh, yes—yes, I do— *(She jots down the address, standing.)*

CHARLES. *(Into phone)*

(ANNABELLE is writing with her eyes on CHARLES.) Yes? You're sure there's no mistake? You see, she was going to— Oh, well, then there couldn't possibly be a mistake, could there? Thank you. *(He hangs up)* She didn't take a cab.

MITCHELL. What is it, sir? Something wrong?

CHARLES. I don't know. My wife planend to visit a friend in New York this afternoon—she isn't there. That was the taxi company—

ANNABELLE. Charles, this is being ridiculous—

CHARLES. *(Overriding her)* She didn't take a cab to the station. She didn't even phone for one.

ANNABELLE. She probably got a lift from someone.

CHARLES. *(Picks up phone, dials Operator)* I suppose that's possible— *(Into phone)* Operator, will you get me the New York Central Station? The ticket office, please.

MITCHELL. Here, let me help you. Tony Coleman's usually on duty this time of day— I'll talk to him.

CHARLES. *(Into phone)* Just a moment. *(Gives phone to MITCHELL.)*

ANNABELLE. Lieutenant, you're as bad as he is!

MITCHELL. *(Into phone)* Hello—Tony? Al Mitchell. I'm up at the Ashton place. Did Mrs. Ashton—you know, Connie Barnes—take a train to New York this afternoon— Have you been behind the window all the time? You sure you know Connie Barnes, Tony? Look, if she was late and had to buy her ticket on the train— I see. Okay, thanks. *(Hangs up, frowning)* Mrs. Ashton didn't get on any train for New York City this afternoon.

ANNABELLE. Now how can your friend be so positive of that?

MITCHELL. Tony can see the platform from the back window of his office. Not many people got on a New York train this afternoon—and Connie Barnes wasn't one of them. Tony *is* positive.

CHARLES. So if Connie didn't go to New York—where in hell is she?

ANNABELLE. It's foolish of you to be so concerned.

CHARLES. Concerned! My God, I'm a damned sight more than concerned! Why didn't Connie go to New York? And why is Ricky in such a frenzy about her? What in hell happened here this afternoon! *(He starts for door Right)* Is Ricky still in his room?

ANNABELLE. I think so—

(CHARLES *exits.*)

Oh, dear, I suppose I shouldn't blame Mr. Ashton for being upset, but—

MITCHELL. Aren't you a little "upset," Miss Logan?

ANNABELLE. *(Carefully)* Well, I must admit that Mr. Ashton's worry has affected me, yes.

MITCHELL. Is that all? You told me about the boy's resentment of Mrs. Ashton. Didn't you say he slashed a dress of hers?

ANNABELLE. That was a very naughty thing for him to do.

MITCHELL. And when you punished him, he resented Mrs. Ashton even more?

ANNABELLE. This *is* a very difficult situation, Lieutenant. Children can be a probelm, but for Mr. Ashton to become this alarmed— Mrs. Ashton might very well have got a ride all the way into New York or—

MITCHELL. Weren't you alarmed? So alarmed that you didn't go to Mrs. Walworth's? You didn't want to leave Ricky and Mrs. Ashton alone together.

ANNABELLE. That's true, but—

MITCHELL. What were you afraid of? Weren't you afraid that the boy might hurt Mrs. Ashton?

ANNABELLE. *(Shocked)* Hurt her? Oh, no— I thought there might be some unpleasantness—and as it turned out, there was. But`I'm sure it was nothing important. You see, I've known little Ricky so well, for so long—

MITCHELL. What was in that letter?

ANNABELLE. *(Turning to* MITCHELL, *startled)* Letter?

MITCHELL. The one from your friend—Lucinda Marsh. Why did you take it?

ANNABELLE. But I didn't!

MITCHELL. *(Stepping behind desk, opening drawer)* It's in your purse, isn't it? You put it there while Mr. Ashton walked to the car with me. *(Closes drower; sharply)* What's in that letter? Something about the boy?

ANNABELLE. Why, I've not even read the letter!

MITCHELL. Has Ricky ever been in trouble before? *(Going to her)* Has he ever hurt anyone? Is there something about that in the letter?

ANNABELLE. You're imagining all of this—

MITCHELL. I don't think so. That's what you're afraid of—that he's hurt Mrs. Ashton. And you're trying to protect him—

CHARLES. *(Offstage Right)* Ricky!

(RICKY *runs in, with* CHARLES *after him.)*

RICKY. *(Running for terrace)* No! I won't answer any more questions!

MITCHELL. Ricky!

RICKY. *(Stops)* Who are you!

MITCHELL. *(Going to* RICKY) My name's Al Mitchell, Ricky. Listen, son, we're worried about your mother—

RICKY. My mother!

CHARLES. *(To* MITCHELL*)* Connie.

MITCHELL. We're worried about Connie, Ricky. Maybe you can help us.

RICKY. *(Frightened)* Are you a policeman?

MITCHELL. I'm a detective, yes—

RICKY. *(To* CHARLES*)* You called the police—

ANNABELLE. Here, let me— Look at the state this child's in! *(Takes* RICKY *by arm)* Ricky, dear, we'll go up to my room, just you and I.

MITCHELL. Just a moment, please—

CHARLES. *(Comes to* RICKY; *calmly now)* Rick, I'm sorry I shouted at you, I'm sorry I frightened you. But I don't know where Connie is—

RICKY. I don't know anything about her! She went to New York!

CHARLES. No—she didn't get on the train. She didn't even call a cab. We checked.

RICKY. She did go to New York. She did!

CHARLES. Did you see her leave? Did you say good-bye to her?

RICKY. No, but she went!

CHARLES. She wouldn't leave without saying good-bye to you.

RICKY. She didn't say good-bye on purpose! Because she broke her promise to me!

CHARLES. What did she promise you?

RICKY. *(Turns away, tight-lipped)* Nothing.

MITCHELL. Ricky, where were you when she left?

RICKY. Up in my room.

MITCHELL. Can you see the driveway from there? Did you see a car?

RICKY. No, I didn't see anything. But when I came down she was gone.

CHARLES. You're so sure of that—why are you so sure?

RICKY. *(Turning to* CHARLES*)* I yelled for her and when she didn't answer, I went looking for her. I looked everywhere and then I knew she was gone when I went and looked—

CHARLES. Went and looked where?

RICKY. No place!

CHARLES. *(Going to him)* What did you see? Where did you look?

RICKY. I won't tell you. I'm not going to be punished again.

MITCHELL. Why should he be punished?

ANNABELLE. The poor child—please—

MITCHELL. Where isn't he allowed to go?

ANNABELLE. Why don't you leave him to me—

CHARLES. *(To* ANNABELLE*)* Is there someplace he's not allowed to go? *(To* RICKY*)* Connie's room—is that it? Is it Connie's room you're not allowed— *(Drops on one knee before* RICKY*)* Did you go into Connie's room? I give you my word you won't be punished. This is more important than that. You went into Connie's room and you saw something—something that made you think Connie had gone. What was it, Ricky?

(CHARLES *grabs* RICKY, *who pulls away and backs into* MITCHELL, *who stops him.)*

Don't be frightened, Rick— I know you didn't do anything wrong—whatever you did was okay. I'm sure it was.

RICKY. *(Pauses. Turns to* MITCHELL, *who stares silently at him. He turns back to* CHARLES*)* All I did was look in her closet! She was going to wear her best clothes to New York and I just looked in her closet to see if her fur coat was gone!

CHARLES. Her fur coat?

RICKY. It's the best of all her clothes. It's the story of her life—and it's gone.

CHARLES. And you think she wore it to New York—on a day like this?

RICKY. She did!

CHARLES. But it's hot as blazes today—

RICKY. She took her fur coat! Look for yourself!

CHARLES. *(Slowly)* No. She was going to put it away— *(Pause)* She was going to store it— *(He turns slowly toward the vault.)*

ANNABELLE. *(Quickly)* No, Charles, she changed her mind—she took it into New York to have it altered—

CHARLES. *(Going to vault)* She might have put it in the vault— *(Opens outer doors, tries steel door.)*

ANNABELLE. No, I spoke to her yesterday about storing it, but there was some work she wanted done first---

CHARLES. *(Going to desk)* The combination, it's in the desk—

(MITCHELL *goes up to vault, examines door.* RICKY *turns to watch* CHARLES *at desk.)*

ANNABELLE. Yes, it's in the top drawer. Now you'll see how absurd you're being—

CHARLES. *(Searching for it)* Annabelle, where is it!

ANNABELLE. Right there—it's always been there.

CHARLES. You know the combination—

ANNABELLE. No. No, I've never known it.

MITCHELL. *(Stepping away from vault)* Doesn't anyone remember the combination?

(A pause.)

ANNABELLE. Ricky, dear, go upstairs.

CHARLES. Yes, Ricky, go upstairs.

(RICKY *exits Right; closes the door, but not completely.)*

It isn't here— I can't find it—

MITCHELL. Somebody must know the combination!

CHARLES. No! It's always been here in the desk—

(MITCHELL *goes to phone and dials Operator.)*

ANNABELLE. Lieutenant, listen to me! She couldn't be in there! She couldn't have opened the vault!

MITCHELL. *(Into phone)* Get me the police—quickly—

ANNABELLE. She doesn't know the combination!

CHARLES. *(Slowly, reasoning it out)* The combination was on a paper in the desk. It's gone now. She could have found it and used it—taken it into the vault with her—

MITCHELL. *(Into phone)* This is Mitchell— Emergency!

ANNABELLE. *(To* MITCHELL) Of course, you're right. We must make sure.

MITCHELL. *(Into phone)* Emergency—at the Ashton place— Charles Ashton, up on the hill— We're afraid someone is locked in a vault—that's right—get the Emergency Squad here immediately— Right. *(He hangs up.)*

CHARLES. How soon can they get here?

MITCHELL. Ten minutes—maybe sooner.

CHARLES. Thank God!

ANNABELLE. Lieutenant, how long will it take to get it open?

MITCHELL. I don't know. It won't be easy. How thick are those walls?

CHARLES. Fourteen inches—sixteen maybe—

MITCHELL. It could take hours—

> (ANNABELLE *turns away in relief.* CHARLES *slowly turns toward vault, rises and quickly goes to it, listening at door.)*

How big is that vault?

CHARLES. *(Turning to* MITCHELL*)* About four by four —seven feet high—

MITCHELL. How long could she have been in there?

CHARLES. I don't know—we left here at three—

MITCHELL. *(Looks at wristwatch)* Five-thirty— *(Almost to himself)* They'll have to work fast!

CHARLES. I don't understand how it happened. How could anyone get caught in there? That door can only be locked from the outside. *(Going to* ANNABELLE*)* Annabelle, maybe you're right—she isn't in there— She couldn't have locked herself in there!

ANNABELLE. Of course not! Charles, stop torturing yourself—

MITCHELL. Exactly; someone would have had to lock her in!

CHARLES. *(Slowly)* What did you say?

MITCHELL. She would have to be— *(He stops, seeing* CHARLES' *reaction.)*

CHARLES. *(Goes slowly to desk, picks up letter)* Connie's dog—it suffocated—

ANNABELLE. Charles, what are you thinking—

MITCHELL. *(Takes letter from* CHARLES. *Looks at it)* Her dog was suffocated? *(Goes to* ANNABELLE) That's what you were hiding—the boy put the dog in the vault— *(Suddenly)* Then he knows the combination!

ANNABELLE. No! No, he doesn't—

MITCHELL. Get him down here—

ANNABELLE. He didn't do it! He didn't kill the dog!

MITCHELL. Get the boy down here!

ANNABELLE. Ricky doesn't know how to open the vault!

MITCHELL. Then how was it opened?

ANNABELLE. He had nothing to do with it! I left it open—it was stupid of me! It was my fault the dog died—entirely my fault!

MITCHELL. Look, Miss Logan—

RICKY. *(In doorway Right)* It wasn't your fault!

(ALL *turn to him.*)

ANNABELLE. Ricky!

RICKY. *(Runs to* ANNABELLE) Don't you take the blame, Miss Annabelle! *(He hugs* ANNABELLE *protectingly)* You leave her alone. She didn't do it, I did it!

CHARLES. *(Goes to* RICKY) Ricky, Connie is in the vault—

RICKY. I didn't do anything to Connie! I didn't shut her in! I didn't do anything to her!

CHARLES. Unless we get her out of there, she'll die. You don't want that to happen, do you?

RICKY. I didn't do it! I didn't do it!

CHARLES. You know the combination! Open the door, Ricky!

RICKY. *(Sobbing wildly, he flings himself at* CHARLES, *beating his fists against* CHARLES'S *chest)* You'll blame me for it. You blame me for everything. You'll blame me! *(He continues sobbing.)*

CHARLES. *(Holding* RICKY *in his arms)* Oh, God!
      (Distant SIREN in heard.)
It's all right, Ricky. It's all right. Whatever happened—You didn't mean it, I know. Now, now— You didn't mean

it. Of course you didn't.
(He walks with his arm around RICKY *toward the vault. The SIREN is heard, closer.)*
Now we'll get Connie out of there and everything will be all right. Now Ricky, you know the combination. Let's open the vault.
(They are in front of the vault.)
What's the first number, Ricky?

(ANNABELLE *moves slowly to where she can see the vault when it opens.)*

RICKY. Twenty-eight—
CHARLES. Do it, Ricky—
RICKY. First you turn it to twenty-eight—
CHARLES. And then? Do you turn it back?
RICKY. Yes—back to eleven—like that—wait, first twenty-eight—back to eleven—and thirty-two—that's it, there!

(RICKY *steps back and* CHARLES *wrenches open the vault door.* CONNIE *stumbles out;* CHARLES *catches her. SIREN is heard coming nearer.* MITCHELL *helps* CHARLES *lift* CONNIE *into his arms.* CHARLES *carries her to the sofa.* CONNIE *leans against the back of the sofa, her eyes closed, gasping for air.* RICKY *runs to* ANNABELLE.*)*

RICKY. Is she all right, will she be all right—
MITCHELL. *(At* CONNIE'S *side)* Yes, she'll be all right.
(The SIREN stops outside. MITCHELL *exits.)*
CONNIE. *(Whispering)* Ricky—
CHARLES. *(Turns away from* CONNIE *to* RICKY; *beckons him to them)* Ricky—
ANNABELLE. *(Goes to table behind the sofa)* Some brandy—
RICKY. *(Kneels before* CONNIE*)* Connie, tell them I didn't do it, please, tell them—
CONNIE. *(Taking* RICKY *in her arms)* No, Ricky, you didn't do it. It wasn't you. It wasn't you—

(Another SIREN in the distance is heard. ANNABELLE *slips quickly into the vault, pulls the door almost completely closed after her.)*

CHARLES. *(Rising slowly from sofa)* Annabelle—
   (MITCHELL *enters, followed by a* POLICEMAN *in uniform.)*
Annabelle! She's gone!
   (MITCHELL *runs out the hall door; the* POLICEMAN *runs out the terrace doors.)*
(CHARLES *starts for the door Right, then stops. He looks at* CONNIE, *then at the vault. He goes to the vault)* Keep this damn door locked! *(He slams shut the steel door, locks it and closes the louvered doors)* I'll have it sealed up tomorrow— *(He starts toward* CONNIE *and* RICKY.*)*

CURTAIN

SPEAKING OF MURDER

PROPERTY PLOT AND CHECK LIST

Special Check Items

All doors open at rise
Vault door shut, handle up
Louvered doors closed
Dog on sofa
Thread off Left louvered door

Pre-Set

Armchair down Left of desk
Desk Left on marks. *On it:*
    Desk blotter
    Dial phone with long cord
    Ashtray with leather base
    Roll-type desk blotter
    Packet of loose notepaper
    Desk pen in holder
    Pipe
    Bronze humidor with tobacco
    Flip-type phone file
    Antique inkwell set
    2 pencils in inkwell tray
    2 dip-type pens in inkwell tray
    Note (reminder of phone call) on desk blotter
    Letter opener on down Right corner of desk
    Pair of scissors on up Right corner of desk
    Opened letter with Cunard Line ticket down stage of
        phone
    2 long white envelopes in Right drawer
    Bunch of loose paperclips in Center drawer
    Bunch of assorted bills and papers in all drawers
    Brown waste basket under Right edge of desk

Cane-bottomed chair up stage of desk on marks
Doorknob set on top cupboard door
Key in cupboard door
Cupboard unlocked
Tall flowers in vase on hall table
Gilt-framed soldier picture on hall table
2 small pewter urns on hall table
Wooden end table Left of sofa. *On it:*
    Ashtray with water
    Book of matches
    Double-easel picture frame with male tintypes
Upholstered armchair Center stage on marks
Overstuffed sofa, slightly angled down Right on marks
2 gray pillows on sofa
Coffee table down stage of sofa. *On it:*
    Ashtray with water on up stage Left coffee table
    3 magazines Center on coffee table
    Gold and ceramic Ronson lighter up Right Center
    Gilt cigarette box with cigarettes and matches up
        Right
End table Right of sofa. *On it:*
    Gold ashtray with water
    Gilt-framed female tintype
    Green base cupid lamp with round shade
    Book of matches
Wingback chair down Right. *On it:*
    Book
Library ladder behind chair
Lectern with large dictionary open on it upstage of wing-
    back chair
Small table under stairs. *On it:*
    4 brandy glasses
    Decanter of brandy

Pre-Set off Left

7 unopened letters with cancelled stamps (ANNABELLE—
    Act One)

   3 to CHARLES
   2 to CONNIE
   2 to ANNABELLE
Roll of architect's plans (CHARLES—Act Two)
6 pages of typed list of names (ANNABELLE—Act One)
Round silver serving tray with doily (MILDRED—Act One)
2 glasses of gin and tonic (MILDRED—Act One and RICKY
  Act One)
Screwdriver (CHARLES—Act Two)
Keyring with several keys (CHARLES—Act Two)
Bankbook in case (RICKY—Act Two)
Bunch of artificial gladiolas (MRS. WALWORTH—Act
  Two)
Rolleiflex camera with neck strap (CHARLES—Act Three)
White yachting cap (CHARLES—Act Three)
Pirate's flag (CHARLES—Act Three)
Typed business letter and addressed envelope (CHARLES
  —Act Two)
Paint rag (JANIE—Act One)

Pre-Set off Right

Clock chime effect with hammer by hall
Door slam by hall entrance
Slashed dress (MILDRED—Act Two)
Green stole (JANIE—Act One)
Green purse (JANIE—Act One)
Pair of white gloves (JANIE—Act One)
Mink coat (ANNABELLE—Act Two)
Bunch of fern
Silver metal vase
Gold and rhinestone cigarette case in CONNIE's *purse*
  (CONNIE—Act One)
Pinwheel on stick (JANIE—Act Three)
Gas-filled balloon on light string (JANIE—Act Three)
Blue air-mail letter (MITCHELL—Act Three)
Pocket notebook (MITCHELL—Act Three)
Roll of architect's blueprints

Act One Personal Props

Paint rag (RICKY)
Ball-point pen (CHARLES)
Blue airmail letter (MRS. WALWORTH)

End of Act One, Scene I

Clear:
> Gin and tonic glass from coffee table
> Book from desk

Set:
> Up stage desk chair on marks

Check:
> Vault and louvered doors closed
> CHARLES onstage on down Right sofa
> Up Left off stage voices in position

End of Act One Scene II

Clear:
> Mail from desk
> Gin and tonic glass from desk
> tall flowers from hall table
> Cigarette case from coffee table
> Coral jacket to off stage

Set:
> Red and what flowers on hall table
> Newspaper on Left end of desk
> Straighten sofa pillows
> Clean and water ashtrays
> Notepapers and pencils on desk
> Lavender sweater for ANNABELLE
> Beige purse hanging on top of take-off stairs
> Scissors with small green thred on blades on top of take-off stairs
> CONNIE'S purse with cigarette case on top of take-off stairs
> 3 pages of script on top of take-off stairs

Check:
> Furniture on marks

Terrace doors open
Hall doors open
Vault and lovered doors closed

End of Act Two, Scene I

Clear:
Newspaper from coffee table
Green dress from Center chair
Cupboard from ANNABELLE
Set:
Desk chair six inches Left
Check:
Cupboard locked
No flower stems showing outside cupboard
CHARLES by up Left terrace door
CHARLES' jacket hanging on back of up stage desk
    chair
JANIE off up Left terrace
Vault and lovered doors closed

End of Act Two, Scene II

Clear:
Gladiolas from cupboard
Screwdriver from desk drawer
Scissors in sheath to up Right corner of desk
Double easel pisture from Left end table
Set:
Glass of water on off Left prop table
Hall doors closed
Beige purse Left on desk
Key back in cupboard door
Cupboard unlocked
Blueprints on hall table
Gladiolas in vase—Right on coffee table
Fern—Center on coffee table
2 gladiolas—Left on sofa table, stems upstage
Letter from veterinarian—Center, on desk

Check:
  Vault doors closed
  Hall doors closed
  Cupboard unlocked
  Property man standing by for clock strike
  ANNABELLE in hall outside hall doors
  JANIE off up Right
  CHARLES off up Left
Personal Props:
  Pencil and whistle (MITCHELL)

SPEAKING OF MURDER

COSTUME PLOT

Annabelle

Act One

Coral dress (Scene I)
Beige shoes (Scene I)
Coral jacket (Scene II)

Act Two

Blue dress
Blue shoes
Lavender sweater
Beige purse

Act Three

Red housecoat
Pair red mules

Connie

Act One

Lilac dress with polka dots (Scene I)
Tan shoes (Scene I)
Green dress (Scene I)
Green stole (Scene II)
White gloves (Scene II)
Green purse (Scene II)
Tan leather purse (Scene I)
Green shoes (Scene I)
Kid gloves (Scene I)

Act Two

White print dress
Cocoa shoes

Act Three

Same as Act Two

MRS. WALWORTH

Act One

Black dress
Black ribbon
Artificial rose
Black purse
Black shoes with red heels
Large black hat with flowers
Black stole with silver thread

Act Two

Dark striped dress
Rest same as Act One

MILDRED

Act One

Gray maid's uniform with white collar and cuffs
Whate maid's cap
White shoes

Act Two

Same as above

Act Two, Scene II

Pink blouse
Brown skirt
Brown shoes

Janie

Act One

Gray flannel shorts
Yellow T-shirt
Yellow T-shirt with paint
Brown belt
Brown shoes
Short white socks

Act Two, Scene I

Khaki shorts
Brown belt
Green and gray T-shirt
Brown shoes

Act Two, Scene II

White shrug
Green dress
White socks
Brown and white saddle shoes
White gloves
White and clear plastic purse

Ricky

Act One

Sneakers
Yellow and green striped T-shirt
Khaki trousers
Brown belt

Act Two, Scene I

Gray jeans
Green T-shirt
Brown loafers

Act Two, Scene II

White shirt

Red tie
Grey flannel trousers
Brown belt
Navy blue jacket
White handkerchief

Act Three

Gray jeans
Green T-shirt
Sneakers
Brown belt

MITCHELL

Act Three

Dark blue suit
Black shoes
Dark felt hat
White shirt
Dark blue tie
Dark socks

POLICEMAN

Act Three

Navy blue cotton shirt
Navy blue wool trousers
Policeman's hat
Black shoes
Dark socks

CHARLES

Act One, Scene I

Dark jacket (black with brown stripe)
White shirt
No tie
Gray flannel trousers
Dark brown suede shoes

Act One, Scene II

Dark navy blue silk suit
White shirt
Dark tie
Handkerchief
Black shoes
Dark socks

Act Two, Scene I

Dark gray trousers
Brown suede shoes
Blue striped shirt
Dark tie
Beige jacket

Act Two, Scene II

Same as Scene I

Act Three

Same as Act Two

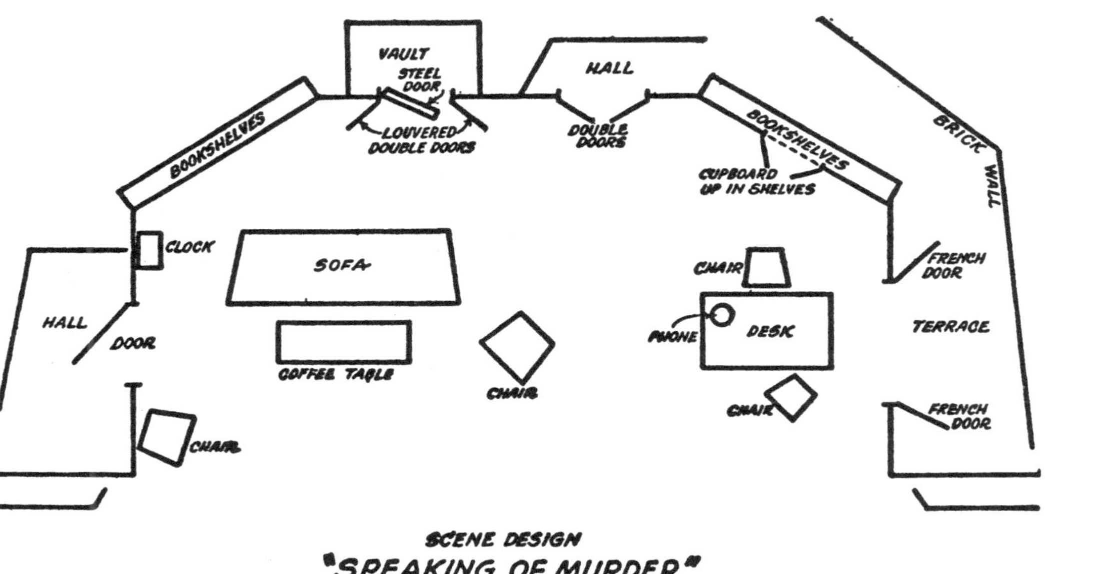

SCENE DESIGN
"SPEAKING OF MURDER"

MUSIC USE NOTE

Licensees are solely responsible for obtaining formal written permission from copyright owners to use copyrighted music in the performance of this play and are strongly cautioned to do so. If no such permission is obtained by the licensee, then the licensee must use only original music that the licensee owns and controls. Licensees are solely responsible and liable for all music clearances and shall indemnify the copyright owners of the play(s) and their licensing agent, Samuel French, against any costs, expenses, losses and liabilities arising from the use of music by licensees. Please contact the appropriate music licensing authority in your territory for the rights to any incidental music.

IMPORTANT BILLING AND CREDIT REQUIREMENTS

If you have obtained performance rights to this title, please refer to your licensing agreement for important billing and credit requirements.